THE WEDDING PARTY

ALSO BY JEAN MARTIN

COMING SOON

Ginny Martin
A Love Through Time

Visit **www.jeanmartin.co.uk** for more information about
the author and new releases.

Visit the link below for her book list:

WWW.JEANMARTIN.CO.UK/BOOKS

THE WEDDING PARTY

WHAT HAPPENED IN VEGAS?

JEAN MARTIN

MISTY
MOON
PUBLISHING

For

My daughters Elizabeth & Victoria
For their love and support
&
Laura Wilkinson
For giving me the confidence to believe in myself

CONTENTS

1

DEPARTURE! VEGAS HERE WE COME!

The Girls.

Four girls, all over twenty-one (so technically women) were off to Vegas for THEE hen party of the century. No one was going to beat it. EVER!

And why is that you say? Well, because the groom and his Stags were going to be there too.

Weird.

Right?

Chief Hen spends weekend partying with Head Stag at same Bachelor (ette) party because they are both insanely crazy at parties and are (quotation fingers)

'Just looking after their assets.'

Hers' being his crown jewels.

His being her lovely booty and err, booties.

They would be travelling separately; of course, to give the celebrations their formal titles of Hen or Stag weekend; they would be sharing the same aircraft, but not the same row of seats.

Or the same stewardess or, usually, not the same toilets.

Yeah. Really weird!

So, Georgia Heinz was leading her gaggle of hens through the terminal towards the check in (yes, I know, geese but please go with the flow.) and looking very prim and proper in her neatly pressed mint trousers and minty, spotted buttoned blouse. Her entourage, or at least two of them, were dressed accordingly, but in different colours, giving the effect of a walking collection of meringues the kind of which were usually found in the freezer aisle of a supermarket, boxed and ready to eat after one hours defrosting. The third 'Hen' was not so delicately dressed, preferring, instead, a good sturdy pair of jeans, a washed-out shirt and scuffed boots for her eight-hour plus flight to America and, ultimately, Las Vegas.

"Dear Lord Georgia! What on earth is she wearing?" Laura Taylor wore a look of disgust as her eyes ran over the under dressed and, in her opinion, unworthy female ever to be blessed with the title Chief Bridesmaid.

Georgia glanced at her soon to be sister-in-law and smiled "Shabby Chic, Laura. Shabby Chic."

"Just plain shabby if you ask me." Laura whispered as she brought her suitcase to a grand stop and dropped the handle as she asked,

"Are the guys here yet?"

"No Laura they are NOT here yet! And if they were here, we're not to mingle, we agreed on that remember?"

This answer came from Millie, the fourth Hen in the party, who was still waiting for the jury's verdict on Laura and her acid tongue.

(The jury was, of course, the one sitting in judgement in her own head and not in a courtroom of law. 'Yet!')

"I know, I know." Laura frowned as she gripped the handle of her suitcase and flicked her wrist to move it several inches to her left.

"Mingling is okay Millie" Georgia smiled "But sex is not! Just remember, NO SEX WITH THE STAGS it's the number one rule above all the others... now let's check in."

~

The Boys.

"Are you sure it's what we should be doing? I mean. It's a Stag do, right?

Aren't we supposed to be sharing the love and getting shit faced while doing, them? I mean, it?"

This came from Ashley Moore. He was vaguely handsome and whippet thin and his plan was, he said, to get laid as often as possible in the next three nights before a long period of drought was forced upon his handsome physique.

"I promised I'd make sure the girls were all looked after this weekend."

Rob Carter said as his shoulders raised in a quick shrug.

"Sorry guys didn't think." He added with a grimace.

"Because you don't have to worry about it!" said Ashley with a fiery look.

"Whaay me neither!" two voices chorused as the owners gave Ashley a hostile glare...

"He's right Rob." Bertie Hicks shrugged "It's a stag do where we should all be getting drunk, puking a lot and losing our watches and wallets and..." He pointed at Ashley "His virginity... These things have just disappeared because we've been reduced to babysitters."

"I doubt that. These girls are party animals." Rob grinned and cringed inwardly at his blatant lie.

"Believe me when I say they'll do anything with you except one thing. YOU don't do it with THEM, and THEY don't do it with YOU. You want sex you go find someone who is not a friend of Georgia's."

He glared at his rut of Stags (bachelors)as he put his hand inside his jacket and pulled out a selection of photos.

"Here they are" he said as he fanned out the three photos that had been squeezed into his pocket.

"The devils in the bodies of women and you, my friends, are their guardian Angels." He gave a mock bow as he offered the photos to whomsoever had the courage to take one, and when they all had one safely in their hands, he grabbed the handle of his suitcase and headed for the check in.

By the time they got to the wall of flight boards, each man had a photograph in his pocket. Alex Sterling, it was bemoaned, had managed to swing the cherry on the cake, Laura Taylor, while Ashley had been left with C.J. (Aka. Penelope Craig.) a calamitous female who would find a bruise somewhere and break something somewhere else.

(She was also Robs' sister, well half-sister, but no one knew that except Georgia, and she wasn't going to tell anyone.)

∼

The women were standing in the check in area, in a huddle of coloured cottons and suitcases, all eyes on the screen as they searched for their flight number and gate. Suddenly the group got bigger as the guys joined them and swung their eyes up to the board too.

"It's too early for this shit!" Laura Taylor complained as her eyes travelled over the board. "Just get me to my seat and let me sleep."

"I'm going to the loo." C.J. smiled then stepped back and disappeared with a yelp. Three minutes passed before she opened her eyes and looked up at several pairs of eyes looking down at her.

"You okay Penny?" Georgia whispered quickly when Penny opened her eyes.

"Yes, I'm fine." Penny sat up. "What happened?"

"You fell over!" Millie's mouth did a quick movement to the right then relaxed.

"I did?"

Everyone nodded.

"How?"

"There was a suitcase behind you, and you fell over it when you stepped back." Georgia glanced at the case that was lying flat on the floor then flicked her eyes up at the collection of friends assembled around them.

"Oh Okay. Was it mine?" Penny asked as she raised a hand to the back of her head.

"No baby it wasn't yours, someone put it there." Georgia slipped a hand under Penny's arm and helped her up. "Are you sure you're, okay?"

Penny gave a nod of her head then grimaced.

"I'm going to go to the bathroom." she murmured as she headed off in the direction of the lady's loo sign that was attached to the wall thirty yards away.

"I'll come too...." Georgia ran to catch up and swung an arm up to Penny's shoulder.

"Your head okay Pen?" she asked as Penny rubbed the sore spot on the back of her skull and squinted against the pain that the action induced. But she nodded that she was okay, because that's what she did; she always said that she was fine even when she was far from it.

"I feel so stupid."

Penny looked at Georgia's reflection in the mirror and shrugged.

"I'm really not such a mess you know! I can go a whole week without falling over and hurting myself."

"I know baby."

"If people just gave me room, I'd be fine, I mean, who puts a suitcase behind someone and expects them not to fall over it?"

Georgia shrugged.

"No Georgia, not a statement, who put the damned suit-case behind me and made me fall over it?"

Georgia frowned and said "Alex Sterling. I think. But several of us have the same case."

"Who is...?"

"Alex Sterling? He's a long-time friend of Robs. Don't really know him, never seen him before. But he looks great."

"I'm sure he does but looking great doesn't make up for being stupid."

Penny washed her hands then turned away from the mirror and left the room.

She had that, I'm up for a fight and I know who I'm going to stick it to, look on her face, which always put Georgia on the alert.

"Penny! please don't, not this weekend. Please!"

Penny didn't stop walking but she did slow down.

"Okay, I won't. But keep him away from me, do that and I won't talk to him, or hit him or even look at him."

"Okay Pen. No close up contact with Alex. I promise."

Penny gave a quick nod of her head, then winced as they made their way back to the others.

The plane had taken off and had been cruising for a couple of hours when Georgia came back from a long visit to the toilet. She was smiling and somewhat red in the face but quite calm when she sat down.

"You Okay Georgie?" Millie asked without raising her eyes from her magazine.

"Yes." Georgia smiled "It's really quite invigorating."

"What is?" Laura sounded bored, and probably was.

"Never mind." Georgia went even redder as she tried to clear her throat while ignoring the several sets of eyes staring at her.

"I've been speaking to Rob."

"Yeah, and you took your sweet time. I had to go find

another loo. Nearly wet myself when I fell over his damn feet sticking out in the aisle like two great lumps of tar. I hurt his toes, he said, but what did he hurt of mine?"

Penny was looking at Georgia with wide angry eyes.

"What were you doing that took you THAT long Georgia!?"

"We. I. err." Georgia's' tongue tangled on her words as her eyes remained glued to Penny's face.

"Oh. My. God!" Laura was looking at Georgia with awe and barely concealed envy. "I've always wanted to do it up here! Divvy up girl, tell us what it was like."

"No! No! No!" Penny pushed herself out of her seat and tugged at the hem of her shirt as she calmed herself.

"I can't listen to this! Sex and airplanes don't mix!"

"God you're such a prude C.J." Laura gave a snort as she pointed a well-manicured finger towards Georgia. "Cos Georgia can tell you that that's not true." Then she laughed, as C.J took herself off down the aisle.

"C.J's been a while Georgia, you think she's, okay?"

Millie was fond of C.J and was silently worried because fifteen minutes had passed, and C.J hadn't returned to her seat.

"It's okay Millie, only way off this plane is by parachute and even C.J. is not going to open the door and jump without one." Laura grinned then took another sip of her drink. "And she's hardly having knock out sex miles above the ground cos she wouldn't know how to do it anyway.'

"LAURA!"

"Oh, come on girls we all know she's a prude, God, she blushes when couples kiss in the movies."

Another sip of the cold drink slid down Laura's' throat as her eyes looked towards the window next to her.

"I think we all need to be careful." She murmured through half closed lips.

"I think we need to be ready for her advances. Because I think C.J is gay."

The words dropped into the air between the women and just like that Millie's decision was made. The jury had been out and come back with their verdict. Laura was nasty. Laura was unpleasant. Laura was going to be trouble to C.J and Millie wasn't going to allow it. She was going to keep an eye on the over indulged, overly self-invested, nastily tongued Laura and keep C.J safe from her.

"I'll go look for her!" Millie got up and started towards the back of the plane.

"I'll go too." Georgia got up and fixed a look on Laura that didn't reflect what she thought about what the woman thought.

"Don't touch my drink Laura I'm sure I'll need it when I get back."

They found C.J. Sitting in a seat with her leg lying in someone's lap, her boot on the floor and a damp cloth wrapped around her ankle. She was also holding a crisp looking white hankie up to her left eye.

"What the hell! Rob?" Georgia settled two very angry eyes on her fiancé.

"She tripped." Offered the fiancé with a shrug of his broad shoulders.

"She tripped!"

(Not a statement, not a question, something kind of between the two.)

"Over what? This is a plane for god's sake, everything loose and hazardous is stashed overhead, what is there to trip over?"

"Err,"

(Lame, as an answer it was sooo lame.)

"Someone stuck the Err word in the middle of the aisle and she tripped over it?"

"Now you know that's not it Georgie."

"Then tell me what it is Rob, and I might calm down. You do want me calm, don't you?"

"It's my fault." Alex Sterling put up a hand in admission. "She came rushing down the aisle and I couldn't move them quick enough, so she went over them."

"Them?" Georgia's eyes flicked over everyone, and she knew she wasn't going to like their excuse for an answer.

"His feet."

Penny took the hankie away from her eye, looked at it then stuck it back on her eyebrow.

"His dumb feet were in the aisle. A-gain!"

"You would have seen them if you'd looked!" Alex wasn't helping with his calm assurance that he had done nothing wrong.

"Oh, I looked alright"

Penny glared at him,

"But then some dumb fool moved as I was stepping over them and I caught my foot on his size twelve's! How hurt shall I get before you're satisfied?"

C.J removed her legs from whoever had lent her his lap and then replaced her sock and boot mumbling every second it took her to do it and then she hobbled back up the aisle to her seat.

"You okay now C.J.?" Millie smiled at her an hour later, but it didn't help.

"Yes! Thank you, Millie, I'm fine."

"You want a coffee or sweet tea?"

"No, I'm going to go mad and have a glass or two of champagne. Then I'm going to go to the loo again and I'm going to stomp on his stupid feet if they are anywhere near the damn aisle."

As it happens, Penny drank the champagne and being a virtual non-drinker, was quickly intoxicated and fell asleep. Meanwhile, back at the Stag area, Ashley thought it was unfair that Alex had put his intended devil into a foul mood and was busy badgering him to exchange photographs, essentially transferring responsibility of the bad-tempered harridan to him and freeing Ashley to pursue the delectable Laura.

It took several hours but by the time the plane landed the transfer was complete.

2

VEGAS FIRST NIGHT AND DAY

They checked in, two to a room. Dumped their suitcases at the bottom of their beds and queued for the showers. Ninety minutes later they'd morphed into pretty girls and handsome men and although they were tired and jet lagged, they were more than a little excited as they descended to the ground floor and went out into the bright lights that were Las Vegas.

C.J thought the lights were entirely too bright, the music too loud and the people too many; and the night was still very young.

They were in the thick of all the afore mentioned music and bright lights when one of the girls motioned that she'd like a drink and within a minute they were all at the bar straining to stay together by resisting the ebb and flow of the people that came and went with their drinks.

They were served quickly, and had downed their first shot with a chorus of noise while making sure another was on the way as they were progressively squashed together in front of a smaller area of the bar counter.

"Drink it C.J!" Georgia held the small glass out to Penny until it was taken, then she downed her own shot and smiled.

"Do I have to Georgia?" Georgia nodded. "I don't want to be sick; you know how I hate that."

"You won't be sick C.J there's hardly any alcohol in it, it's mostly sugar and water."

"Really?"

"Really. Drink."

C.J tipped the glass, filled her mouth with the sweet but burning liquid then frowned because it tasted like all the alcohol in the town, in the world, was in that glass.

"I think I need to go back to the hotel." Penny was grinning, five minutes later, which wasn't a good sign.

"You can't." Georgia's answer was emphatic. "We've only been out an hour and a half, and the karaoke hasn't started yet."

"No!" C.J shook her head

"No, no, no. I am not getting onto a silly little stage and making a spectacle of myself Georgia. I'm very far away from sober and will not get off this chair cos I'm sure to fall over."

"C.J!"

"No Georgia, you go, I'm not a good singer."

"You're the best singer here Penny Craig, you just need Dutch courage to get behind the mike. So come on."

"No, please, Gee-oorg-iia."

Penny tried to disengage her arm, but Georgia was insistent then the air squawked above them and...

"Karaoke is on hold tonight folks" boomed out a male voice.

And it was like he'd said it hadn't ever been invented because there was a collective sound from the unhappy wannabe stars; and a grunt of disapproval from Georgia as she released Penny's arm. Penny breathed a sigh of relief because she really, REALLY, had not wanted to sing anyway.

"Karaoke will kick off again in a couple of hours." Continued the voice "But until then we have something special for you... Coz a bird has flown all the way from the UK to be here tonight... so let's give a big Vegas welcome to Fluffy Flamingooo!"

The place went quiet, so quiet you could have heard a hairpin drop to the floor and rebound off it because twenty seconds after the announcement a six-foot-tall drag queen sashayed onto the floor in front of the silenced karaoke machine then took up a hand on hip pose as she looked back at the crowd that was looking, wide eyed and open mouthed, at her.

And what a sight she was, standing in the cooling breeze from the overhead AC unit as it wafted over her head and onto her shoulders.

Penny's eyes were agog at the sight of her, as were every one else's' because this female performer was dressed in pale lavender from the top of her head to a point just above the yellow ankle boots, she wore. And didn't she look, kind of, darling standing there looking back at everyone with those very large eyes that graced her flawless face.

Dear Lord but she was gorgeous and kind of kooky too because her costume was rather more than a little different to what you'd normally see a Queen wear; the upper portion of her was covered in soft baby feathers while her legs were encased in sheer, lavender coloured stockings that held a slight shine.

The lavender wig she wore was styled to allow some hair to cover her from hair line to eyebrow while baby feathers of the same shade, but varying lengths, had been intricately woven into it and then fluffed up to give her head the overall appearance of a gigantic Dandelion fluff ball. Her eyes had been made to look huge in her face before her eye lashes had been adorned with the finest long black feathers that Penny had ever seen. The skin, nose and cheekbones below those eyes had been dusted with a powder that gave off a delicate sheen and her mouth had been dressed in a bright yellow lipstick that pretty much matched the colour of her boots.

The rest of her attire consisted of a one-piece body suit carefully covered in overlapping soft feathers that seemed to hover over her, quite unexpectedly, shapely body. Her legs were long and wore the sheer tights like they were her own skin and the yellow boots on her feet were of a delicate leather construction and bore the weight of several yellow feathers, lengthwise, down the front of them.

She was immaculate.

She was stunning.

Alex followed Penny to the front of the, now, whispering crowd, where they stood no more than five feet away from the gorgeous Fluffy Flamingo.

Then...

"Oh!" Penny's hand went to her mouth when she saw the delicate diamonds that were balanced on the eyebrow feathers. They were so tiny that they would have been missed if it hadn't been for the constant tilting and flicking of the large eyes. The placement of them, at strategic points on the feathers, allowed for a graceful curve to make them look like they were the eyelashes themselves.

Alex was dumbstruck.

Penny was in awe of the overall effect and the Fluffy herself was quite openly accepting the silence in front of her as if it was the norm where she was concerned.

And then she spoke, and the room echoed with the gasps and nervous laughter that her voice invoked.

"Hello, my darling..." said a deep sultry voice in Penny's direction. "You look very nice tonight... Is he your man?" The dandelion ball dipped in Alex's direction... "I hope not... he needs to improve his choice of nightwear... very basic... very basic...kinda can't be bothered if you know what I mean, which is harsh on you girl, cos you're a pretty one..." The large eyes returned to Alex and "get a grip mate, suits are not what's required when you have such a lovely girl with you... And you, over there!..."

The Flamingo's attention moved to her next victim and when she'd pulled him to pieces, very gently, well kind of, she started interacting with the crowd, sashaying this way and that, flicking her hips out while telling her stories and raucous jokes and generally pointing at people who were caught between joining in with the laughter or leaving the menagerie.

Fluffy left the floor to catcalls and applause as the party returned to the bar where Laura ordered drinks, Millie took a fit of the giggles and Georgia threw herself into the arms of her fiancé and began kissing him like they were the only people in the room.

C.J had made it back to the bar but was swaying gently to and fro and was ordered to sit on the nearest vacant stool to negate the possibility of falling over. These several things occurred within forty-five seconds of Fluffy's exit, in the forty-sixth second Bertie and Ashley joined them at the bar and upset the rudiments of bar queuing that allowed the orderly sale and removal of intoxicating fluids.

During the ensuing melee, where all of them ordered some kind of alcohol and tried to find the money to pay for them, C.J. was caught on the temple by the sharp point of an elbow and was sent crashing to the floor; where she remained for several seconds before a pair of strong hands tucked under her arms and dragged her up again.

"Sorry. You okay Red?" Alex was looking at her with concern, she, meanwhile, was looking at him with murder in her eyes and Georgia was finally coming up for air

"C.J?" Georgia frowned at the look on her friends' face.

C.J had lost it!

"That does it! I'm done. I'm going back to the hotel; I'm

going back and I'm packing my bags and then I'm going to go home." Penny Grumbled.

"Now C.J. you know you can't do that because the plane doesn't leave till Monday evening."

"I'm going to be in a cast by then, that's if he hasn't killed me first!"

"He?"

"Big foot."

"WHO?" Rob and Georgia asked at the same time.

"Never mind. I'm off home, to the hotel. See you tomorrow."

Georgia nudged Rob as they watched her go and, in turn, Rob glared at Alex then dipped his head in Penny's direction.

Alex left.

"Hey."

Penny ignored him.

"Hey!" Alex tried again, "You want some company?"

"Not yours."

"It's dangerous to go off on your own you know?"

"Not as dangerous as it is staying here with you."

"You're drunk."

"So are you."

"Then we'll just have to stagger about together."

Penny paused and squinted at him as if there was a war going on in her head then.

"Okay," she told him "But you have to walk over there." Penny flicked a finger to her left and waited for him to follow its point.

"But that's the road!" Alex murmured.

"Yes... it is."

"Cars go on the road."

"And... so do your feet."

"My feet!" Alex's head was nodding gently but he didn't know it.

"What's up with my feet?" he asked then he smiled at her.

"They tend to get in my way." She told him.

Which made Alex shrug as he looked down at his shoes before he squinted at her and grinned.

"Shall we get a drink? Or some food?" he asked as he stepped in front of her and turned to face her.

He was walking backwards along the path and was managing to miss everything coming the other way; which made Penny think that he was making her life a misery by intent; after all, how could he not hit all those pedestrians behind him yet manage to clock her one on the side of the head when she was right in front of him?

No answer came to that question, so she told him a definite no to the food and fluids then concentrated on putting some space between them.

He kept up; God damn him.

"Well, I'm hungry so I'm getting myself a burger." He told her.

"And fries?" she queried.

"Of course." He kind of grinned at her.

"Okay." She said as she kind of grinned back.

They sat and ate one burger and fries between them and drank a couple of glasses of beer, each taking a mouthful from the same glass until they were empty. Then they stood and were back on the street.

"You cut your face." Alex ran a thumb across the dried line of blood in Penny's eyebrow.

"Yes, thanks for that." She murmured as she dipped her face away from his fingers.

Alex frowned.

"And I have a lump on my head and a bruise on my knees. Thank you for those too."

"Sorry."

"Yeah, well, I still have lots of areas on my body that are

pain free, no doubt you'll change that tomorrow." Penny laughed and Alex joined in as he draped an arm across her shoulders.

"Does it hurt?" He asked quietly.

"They hurt. Yes."

"Come here."

"What!"

"Relax Red and let me kiss it better."

Penny stood still as he brought his lips down and gently touched them to the cut on her eyebrow.

"Okay?" He asked on a whisper and she nodded.

"Good." He whispered as their eyes locked, then he smiled as he brought his mouth down onto hers; and Penny accepted the kiss as the alcohol from the beer worked its way up to her head and his tongue worked its way across her lips.

They spent the next ten minutes one foot inside the alley, with the alcohol working on their senses as their lips worked out on each other.

And all the time Alex was aware of a white flashing light that illuminated the bricks and the floor and them. He turned to look at it and blinked against the incessant flicker; then he frowned because something had appeared in front of it and was blocking out more and more of the light as its shimmering shadow got closer to them.

Then something pink touched his shoulder before moving to the top of his arm and taking a firm hold of his jacket.

Before he knew what he was doing he was pulling C.J. behind him in the direction of a door; and she was following him through it, into the flashy interior.

"My dear Flamingo what are you doing?" asked a quiet voice that belonged to a female of medium height who wore a long sparkling dress that hugged her plump frame like it was stitched onto her. Her dark hair was piled onto the top of her head and a tiara sat in the midst of the beehive and curls.

"I brought you some customers..." answered Flamingo "you said you were bored and needed to marry someone..."

"I don't do straights, and you know it!" huffed the rather attractive female.

"Yeah, I know but you haven't married anyone for a long time; I'm trying to help here Dusti so keep your hive on..."

Fluffy's eyes gave Alex the once over then she turned back to Dusti, smiled, and said,

"He is kinda cute Dust?"

Dusti, gave Alex the once over annnd...

"His face is to die for but the rest of him belongs in a sixties regen flea pit..." she answered as she raised a gloved hand and gently eased a stray lock of hair off her forehead.

"She's talking about you..." Penny told Alex as she grinned at him.

"Yeah..." Alex grinned back.

"Makes me feel a bit left out..." Penny's bottom lip pouted as her eyes slid over Dusti.

"Dusti doesn't do women..." Flamingo gave a toss of her head... "She's strictly male orientated."

"Hmm" Penny's answer was slightly indifferent because she'd suddenly caught sight of the tiara on top of Dusti's head and was more interested in touching it than touching anything else in the room. Alex, on the other hand, who was trying to stay away from the Fluffy person, was beginning to look a little perplexed and about ready to vacate the building.

"I really can't bring myself to do it Fluff" Dusti was flapping a hand in front of her face as she looked at Alex... "it goes against the order of things, I mean, a mixed marriage hasn't been performed here since the vamp vacated the place and its cobwebs."

Dusti poked at the tiara with a gloved hand and set it slightly askew as...

"The vamp... ?" asked Penny valiantly.

"Impersonator... " answered Dusti.

"Is he still alive?" asked Alex as he took a wobbly step nearer the door.

"The vamp aka. Henry Brown, got into trouble with the feds and had to leave PDQ..." explained Dusti "He left his bible and candlesticks on the table and took off with the money I paid him for this place, and I haven't performed a mixed marriage here since."

"Mixed as in Catholic and..."

"Male and female..." interrupted Fluffy quickly "Dusti says she won't do it because straights are just too boring..."

"I'm not boring..." chorused Alex and Penny.

"You're wearing a suit, an almost black suit..." Fluffy's mouth turned itself down then back up again.

"It's charcoal..." Penny's mouth formed a perfect 'o' for a second then she grinned.

"It's fucking awful..." Dusti replied blandly. "Take it off..."

"No..." Alex refused as he grabbed the front of his jacket and pulled it tight against his body. "I can't do that..."

"Why not?" this question came from Penny, surprisingly, "It's a bloody awful thing to be wearing in a cool place like this..."

"Cool, are you nuts..." Alex whispered in surprise.

"I'm not... Nuts..." Penny swayed a little on her feet then tried to right herself.

"I just think that Dusti is right, and I think that Dusti has the most precious tiara I've ever seen."

"You think?" asked Dusti, as she preened and poked at the tiara making the beehive jiggle.

"Oh yes..." sighed Penny "May I have a closer look..."

"Sure..." Dusti pulled Penny over to where a chair stood under a bright light and sat on it then, "Look away lovely girl" she told her before she sat ramrod straight and waited a second before she said...

"I use it as a prop, you know, for the brides, so they look even more beautiful; but no-one comes here anymore so I wear it, it's a sin to have it lying around, so I wear it."

Penny gave Dusti a sad smile then turned her attention to the beautiful headpiece; she saw the empty settings where some stones were missing as she followed the rows of diamonds with a steady finger; then she held her breath as her eyes took in the single pearl suspended on a delicate string of smaller diamonds inside a heart shaped chamber.

"Oh my!" Penny whispered as she allowed the pearl to sit gently on her fingertip... "These are real diamonds, and the pearl..."

"Well of course they're real girl, it belonged to my granny, and she didn't wear no paste!"

"It's old..." Penny purred. "And the setting is a bit dated but it's still in demand, it's beautiful..." Penny smiled down at Dusti "You are a beautiful lady Dusti...I think I like you..."

Dusti's Adams apple rose and fell, and her eyes shone with emotion as she got to her feet...

Then... "Are you sure you like suit boy?" she asked suddenly.

Penny, who was now drunk and gem high, and not really compos mentis enough to realise the effect of her words or actions, grinned as she looked at Alex and confidently said...

"I DO."

Then...

"Hey! Suit boy..."

Alex frowned as he settled wobbly eyes onto Dusti...

Dusti dipped her head in Penny's direction and said... "Do you want her?"

Alex, who didn't stop to evaluate the question, which he would have done if his brain wasn't immersed in alcohol fumes and his common sense hadn't become a rarity, gave a slow nod of his head.

"Nodding don't count..." growled Dusti.

Silence... several seconds of silence...

"You have to say the words..." whispered Fluffy.

"You have to say it..." reiterated Penny who, God love her, didn't really know why she was urging Alex to say anything at all.

"I DO" said Alex with absolute certainty, with absolute confidence, with absolutely no idea what he'd just said, 'I DO' to."

"Do you have a ring, Suit Boy?"

Fluffy asked from the side of him, close at the side of him.

Alex, the Alex who didn't know what the F was going on, not the one who'd refuse to remove the ring from his finger under any circumstances, removed the ring from his left pinkie finger and slid it onto Penny's ring finger left hand.

"I now pronounce you man and wife..." Dusti made a dead pan face at Fluffy and shrugged her shoulders as if to say "why not?" before she pulled the newlyweds towards a white table that had a pile of blank forms, a few pens and several erotic figurines modelled in risqué positions.

Penny's eyes fixed on the well-made figures as Alex took hold of the pen that Dusti had slapped into his hand, then he signed on the dotted line that Dusti's long manicured finger-nail was tapping on.

The pen was quickly removed from Alex's hand and placed into Penny's.

"Sign here!" Dusti told her as her fingernail tapped on a different set of dots.

Penny's eyes diverted long enough to sign her name then deviated back to the figurines...

"Number 27..." crooned Dusti as her finger touched the first ornament...

"48..." Her finger touched the next in line.

"And my absolute fave... number 69..."

"Number 69!" Penny's eyes flicked over the third figurine

then moved to settle on Dusti who was rolling up the signed paper and tying a pink ribbon around it.

Then.

"Take this..." she whispered to Penny. "Take it to a lawyer soon as you get home... make it legal, real quick..."

Penny took the paper.

Alex took her arm.

The door took them back out onto the street.

"You didn't charge them a dollar!" Fluffy told Dusti as she stood in the doorway waving goodbye.

"I couldn't..." Dusti shrugged. "I feel real bad for her... she's a lovely girl, but he's soo... STRAIGHT!"

Fluffy stood nodding her head then did a small pirouette... "shall we celebrate the first you've ever done darling?"

"First?"

"Man, n woman, male n female, straight n straight. You know lovey...."

"Don't remind me bitch.... Never thought I'd sully the place that way...." Dusti gave a long, pained sigh, then smiled.... "Bring over the good stuff Fluff, I made a new friend tonight and I just love who it turns out to be!"

Penny groaned. She heard herself do it and opened her eyes. Then closed them again. Her head hurt. Her face hurt. Her knees hurt. But her feminine bitsss were kind of humming? She pushed her arm inside the covers then lifted said cover with both hands as she glanced down and saw her naked body. She looked at it for a moment then frowned and tipped her head to the right, as if to silently verbalise an 'ok' at the sight of herself so undressed while in bed.

It must have been a damn good night, she decided as she dropped the covers, because she couldn't remember getting undressed and dropping into the bed. Or getting to the bedroom at all. The fact that she was there was a small miracle because when she got drunk, and she had been, she guessed, very drunk, her sense of direction dove past shaky to absolutely abysmal.

She frowned.

She needed to see Georgia.

For an explanation.

But first she needed the bathroom, so she kicked off the covers and was sitting on the edge of the bed when a pain hit her between the eyes. She pushed a thumb onto the painful area and made circles with it to try to get rid of the throbbing, then she blinked and looked about for a wrap or dressing gown; but when neither showed itself she took hold of the sheet and wrapped it around her body before opening the door and heading across the floor.

The sound of the water, hitting the shower guard, was deafening, so maybe the decision to take a shower right then wasn't such a good idea. Her head was starting to pound and her stomach had started to churn. She picked up the gratuity shampoo from the metallic shelf on the wall, dumped a dollop into the palm of her hand and slapped it onto her head. It smelt pretty good, a bit appley and spicy. Oh dear!

Penny returned to the shower pale and shaking.

So much for not being sick! Georgia had a lot to answer for she thought as she re-soaped her body then stood under the power spray and let the water wash it off.

Back in her room she dug a shirt and pair of trousers out from her case, then tossed pants, bra and socks and a hairbrush onto the bed.

Five minutes later she was dressed and ready for the day.

She hoped.

Now she just had to twiddle her thumbs as she waited for the others to surface. Where was her sketchpad because there was still work to do on some designs and measurements to calculate.

And what the hell was that doing on her hand?

On her finger?

On her left ring finger.

How had she not noticed it when she was in the shower, or throwing up... well maybe not then...

She frowned at the thing for almost a minute as she tried to remember what had happened the night before.

Anything?

Anything at all?

But all that surfaced was the damn non-alcoholic shots (yeah, right!) and him, chucking her onto the floor. God help him when she saw him cos, she was going to hit him and damn HARD. Meanwhile, the ring, which she had slipped off her finger, was going to be put somewhere safe and that was on the chain that was always present around her neck. It was strong. It was safe. It was also a mystery where the, actually, old and expensive looking ring, had come from.

∾

"I was sick this morning Georgia."

"Me too." Georgia grinned.

"It's not funny. You said that shot was only sugar and water and so I wouldn't be sick."

"I lied."

"No shit!"

"You need to let your hair down Penny. You're too wound up."

They were in the lift going down to the restaurant, not that she felt very hungry.

"Comes from working with all that wood and metal." Georgia grabbed her arm "makes you all wooden, like a puppet!" she said as she gently shook it.

35

"I'll have you know that wood is a…"

"Beautiful living thing from which lovely things are born. Yes, I know, just don't talk like that in front of the boys, they'll stay away from you like you have the plague."

"The plague was brought to London on a large ship made from wood."

Georgia rolled her eyes.

"Maybe I'll have a word with Big Foot, Georgia. If you're right about the boredom of trees, then a couple of hours talking to him about rings and grain, and he'll be keeping his big feet out of my way saving me all that energy picking myself up off the floor."

"The boys have gone out to play so you won't see him." Georgia said as she slipped a pair of sunglasses onto her nose.

"Really? Where?"

"Don't know, don't care. Let's go to the shops."

The Stags were in a small building full of slot machines enjoying the cool air conditioning; they'd spent the early part of the morning (8am until twenty minutes ago -11:45-) firing guns on a firing range. Not just any old gun either, these ones were either attached to a big chunk of moveable metal, namely a tank, or a large plastic tube that rested on their shoulder.

They should still be there, but they had tired of the repetitive motions of checking ear gear, loading up and pulling the trigger (I know, I know, a tank has rather more about it than a trigger to send its ordinance through the air, but you still have to be interested in it all.)

Anyway, having made several holes in the allotted area of combat they decided to make their way back to humanity and find the girls because you could only cheer so many hits, enjoy so much inner buzz, before it actually became a chore.

(I know, men bored with big gunny things- Go figure.)

The Slot Palace was a cool contrast to the rising heat of the desert. It was alive with winking lights, bells, groaning machines and punters and lots of females walking around with trays in their hands.

"Don't think this is a good idea." Alex frowned as his eyes scanned the interior.

"It's okay Alex, this is Vegas, home of bright lights and slots and wedding parlours." Rob grinned as he motioned to a waitress, put in a drinks order, then turned towards a brightly coloured, flashing slot machine.

"Yeah," mumbled Alex "well I just want to have some money in my wallet when we leave!"

"If it bothers you so much then take a pew by the door, look out at the sunshine while you spin away your fortune." Rob slapped him on the back "meanwhile" he added with a big grin "the real men will be inside soaking up the am-bi-ance."

"You're a dick Rob." Alex grinned.

"Yeah, and you're bound too tight, you need to smell the trees not just sit behind the wood."

"AY?"

"Get from behind your desk, "injected Bertie Hicks, "go to the country and breathe deep, you'll be surprised at how great it smells."

Bertie Hicks actually wiggled his eyebrows after saying something so. So?

Well, whatever it was it was also stupid.

Alex sat at the slot machine nearest the wide entrance, playing with the coins in his hands.

Chink, chink, brrrip as, up in the air, piped music filtered down.

Alex's torso began to sway to the music, and his head began to nod as he raised a hand, put a coin up to the slot and pushed it in with his finger. The wheels went round and stopped. He punched the hold button on three of the five spools then flicked the handle down. The wheels spun. The lights on the machine winked at him and then, when the wheels had stopped spinning, the machine rang and buzzed and flashed and he was a thousand dollars richer.

And that's when he saw them, walking into a boutique on the other side of the road, Georgia and Laura, the other one and C.J.

He watched them disappear then gathered his coins and moved to the slot machine on the other side of the door.

In the fifteen minutes it took for the women to mooch around the inside of the shop and step back out onto the sidewalk his thousand dollars in slot coins had been replaced by paper money and he'd put several coins back into the machine.

Chink, chink, brrrip said the coins in his hand as the girls stepped outside and placed sunglasses onto their noses.

Alex fastened his eyes on C.J who was leaning forward and laughing, she was carrying a smallish paper bag and looked 'very pretty,' he thought, as he pushed a coin into the slot and pulled down the handle.

Alex had kept his eyes on C.J as she walked out of sight, so he had to stand up quickly when a never-ending stream of coins crashed down into the cup in front of him and bells and lights announced a big win.

Five thousand dollars in slot coins. He'd just won another five thousand dollars. He grinned because he liked this. A lot.

Alex collected his prize money then stepped out onto the sidewalk and looked up and down it hoping to see the girls. They were out of sight, so he spent some time drinking coffee and enjoying some alone time before the others stepped out into the warm sunshine and headed for him. He smiled at their long faces and was silently pleased when they set off back in the direction of the hotel.

"Rob! Rob! Over here." Georgia ran up and planted a kiss on Rob's lips.

The other girls moseyed over like the whole thing was getting boring while the men tried not to look down at heart and down in the mouth, because they'd pretty much blown a week's wages on the slots and were now in need of some cheering up.

Not Alex, of course, he was still buoyed from his win, so, to cheer them up, he bought them all a hotdog with varying relish requirements and a soft drink to wash it all down.

"Wow! Six thousand dollars from poking a coin into a slot, you must be so proud!" C.J remarked without a smile.

"Yeah! Lucky guy! I lost a couple of hundred before I saw the light." Ashley looked anything but chagrined by his admission.

"Which light was that?" Laura was squinting at him as she sipped her cola.

"The next machine over." Bertie Hicks grinned.

"Yeah. And the one after that."

"Okay, okay, I admit it I'm a piss poor gambler, but I have high hopes of winning in the end." Ashley admitted.

"Winning what?" Laura placed her cup on the bench and returned her eyes to him.

"The fair maid." He told her as he leaned forward and took an exaggerated bite of his dog.

"C.J? You, okay?" Georgia called across the few feet of ground between herself and Rob's sister.

Penny nodded.

"Excuse her." Laura gave a half smile "she's a tree hugger, a clandestine one, but a hugger just the same."

"Leave her be Laura!" Millie squeezed the words out from around a mouthful of bread and meat.

"Ah, the lover of women speaks!"

"If you're trying to say I love C.J. you're right, she's a gentle soul who wouldn't hurt a fly, but if you're saying I love women in the sexual sense and have an aversion to the male form you're wrong."

"Puh!"

"I can say, hand on heart." Millie put her hand on her heart (just so you know) "that I have had the pleasure with someone standing right here." She looked about her, saw the men were separated from the women by several paces, then pointed at them and said, "I mean over there."

The women gasped and looked at her with wide eyes.

The men looked at each other and tried to stare each other into divvying up.

The sun shone.

Silence reigned.

All eyes turned to Millie.

"I'm not saying." She told them. "And neither will he!" she looked at the collected men and saw the almost indiscernible movement of one head. "So, if you don't believe me tough shit."

C.J. was ignorant of the conversation going on behind her because she'd taken her hot dog and cola over to a large wooden carving that stood in the middle of a patch of dry, coarse sand and was leaning against it as she ran her hand over the smooth grain; then, after a minute or so, she took a sip from her cup as she eased away from the totem and went around behind it where she ran a hand over the rough bark.

"Whatya -do-in?" Alex asked as Penny circled the whole structure, her hand trailing behind her across the surface.

"I just wanted to touch it."

"Why?"

"Because it's beautiful."

"It's old and dirty!"

"To you maybe, to me it's a work of art."

"You are a tree hugger." He laughed and she glared at him.

"I cut trees into..."

"Ahh, you're not a tree hugger you're a lumber jack."

Penny glared at him then said...

"Do me a favour Alex."

"Sure." Alex Shrugged.

"Fuck off."

3

SECOND NIGHT AND DAY

"I can't wear this!"

"You can and you will Penny!"

"Georgia! Please! I feel..."

"What! You feel what!"

"Unclean. A hussy. A ..."

"You look very sexy."

"Oh Lord! Really?"

"Yes, and there's nothing wrong with looking like that! No-one's going to know what's under your dress, just you and me and these four walls...."

Georgia laughed.

Then there was a knock at the door, and she said, "Just wear it" as she pulled her robe closer and walked quickly to answer it.

"Hey baby." Rob slipped his hands inside Georgia's robe as he planted a kiss on her lips. "We came to escort you lady's downstairs."

"We? Who we?"

"Me and Alex"

Georgia waited for both men to enter the room, gave Alex a long quizzical look then said "Okay, won't be long. "before she dropped a kiss onto Rob's mouth and went into her room to dress.

The men stood in silence for several minutes before Rob took a seat and Alex started to pace around the room.

"C.J not out yet?" Georgia asked ten minutes later as she glanced at her friend's door, then headed for it when the men shook their heads.

Then...

"C.J stop being a prude, leave it and get into your dress."

"I cannot wear this thing!" Penny stepped into Alex's line of sight, she was framed by the open door, lit up by the soft light of the bedroom. The body-hugging piece of feminine underwear *WAS* hugging her perfectly lovely feminine form.

"Yes, you can!" Whispered Alex as Georgia said the same words loud and firm.

"They're waiting for us we have to go."

Penny hesitated.

"Come on, you'll forget you've got it on before we hit the ground floor."

So, despite her reservations, Penny did what she was told and stepped into her dress; but when they stepped out onto the ground floor, she still felt uncomfortable, and Alex, being so close to her when she was wearing the sexy piece of lingerie, was, for some reason, *exciting*.

They had separated into couples. Which was weird, considering six eighths of them were supposed to be un-attached and looking for fun; and yet they didn't stray far from each other because they enjoyed each other's company, (Laura excepted of course) and they all knew who drank what alcohol and ate what food and who liked karaoke. So why change a good thing.

By the time the third round of drinks had been consumed,

the rotational sequence and process for the procurement of said alcohol had left the building and chaos had set in.

When the sign went up for the latest demand for drinks everyone congregated at the bar and over ordered the intoxicating beverages. Four guys, four orders too many drinks, not enough bar space, lots of hands moving, shoving, spilling, and knocking. Oops!

C.J felt several things in the space of five seconds:

1. Someone brushed her shoulder with an arm.
2. Someone said shit and tried to stop a glass from tipping over, only to send it over anyway because the fumbling fingers belonged to an incompetent juggler and big footed galoot.
3. Hands were flapping in front of her, on the front of her, trying to get rid of the cold red liquid that was staining her new pink dress and wetting her through to the skin.
4. Her shock was turning to anger, her face was turning towards the fool who'd soaked her, and Georgia was trying to calm her before the storm took flight.
5. Too late! Fuse ignited. Wait for the explosion!

"C.J.! C.J.!" Georgia tried to calm her, but C.J was seeing red, and not just on the front of her dress.

Penny dropped her chin to her chest and puffed out a long, frustrated sigh, then she picked up the nearest glass and downed a double something and cola before sliding off the barstool and attempting to stomp out of the club. But there were too many people between her and the door, so she had to be content with doing the soft shoe shuffle to get passed them and out onto the street.

Alex followed her out and called to her to stop.

"Why?" she rounded on him and fixed him with a filthy glare." You sorry you didn't hurt me this time?"

"I am sorry. It was an accident."

"Yeah, that's what they all say. 'Sorry guv'nor, oi deedn't meen it.' Sniff. 'Me 'and just kind of pooshed it an' then it fell!"

"Very good." Alex held out his hands and clapped.

"You on the stage?" He mocked "Well don't quit your day job kind of comes to mind."

C.J glared at him again.

"Just go away and leave me alone." She told him on a tired sigh, like a whisper of the wind, but he ignored her.

"You want food.?"

"No, I don't want food!"

"You sure you look kind of pale."

"That's because it's dark."

"What?" Alex frowned at her; his eyes wary, his mouth a straight line.

"I turn into a vampire when it gets dark." Penny grinned, "I just lured you out here to drink your blood."

The words were hardly out of her mouth before Alex pulled her to him, tipped back his head and offered her his throat.

"Go ahead" he whispered, his voice smooth and deep, "I dare you."

Penny didn't hesitate, she put her lips against his neck, opened her mouth a quarter of an inch and nipped his skin between her teeth. It was quite tasty skin too all freshly shaved and doused with a subtle aftershave she couldn't name.

(And now there was a small pink spot on his throat where her teeth had nipped together.)

"I'll take that burger and fries if it's still going." She told him when she'd released him and stepped away. "I'm suddenly very hungry."

And I know it's not for beer and chips, Alex Sterling.

"You drunk?" Alex asked her as she nibbled down the length of several fries, a few minutes later.

"Yeah." She grinned and he couldn't take his eyes off her mouth, or the chip sticking out of it.

So, he leaned forward, took the chip into his mouth and managed to touch her lips with his before his teeth cut through it.

Penny's hand came up quickly and pushed him away. There was a frown on her face and uncertainty in her eyes.

"Please, don't do that." She told him.

"Eat a fry?" He questioned quietly.

Penny shook her head. "Take advantage." She replied softly.

"Hmm, if I said I don't do that would you believe me?" Then, his eyes were looking straight into hers and somehow, she was looking straight back.

Penny gave a shrug of her shoulders

"I don't know you" she told him "But I'd like to think you don't"

They lapsed into silence and had been sitting in it for a few minutes when Penny started quietly humming as she finished off the thin chips.

When the last one had disappeared and she'd washed it down with a mouthful of beer, Alex raised the bottle to his mouth, drank the small amount of liquid left inside it then held out his hand as he stood up.

"Where are we going?" Penny asked as she went ahead of him out into the street.

"There's a big machine up the road, you want to share the jackpot?" he was smiling at her so...

"What makes you think you're going to win it?" she asked.

"Because you just told me."

"Huh?"

"That song you're humming, it's a sign."

"A sign?"

"Yeah." He tugged her hand and started to walk up the road.

"Come and be my good luck charm." He said in a flat monotone.

Penny pulled back, and shook her head, but after a moments' hesitation she went with him, because she was tipsy, and relaxed and oh so happy to be his, good luck charm… or not.

"You've put enough cash in it!" she told him a half hour later. "Just face it ay! I'm not lucky and am certainly not a charm."

"Shhh." Alex grinned at her as he dropped another coin into the slot and pulled the handle and when the wheels stopped, he raised his hand to drop another one in.

"WAIT!" Penny grabbed his wrist and brought her eyes to his. Then she swallowed, hard, and stepped closer.

"If this one doesn't win, will you stop?"

"Kiss it." Alex held the coin out to her, and she dropped her lips to it.

"Okay, here it goes." He grinned as his finger and thumb gripped the coin then flicked it into the slot.

Slow motion. Everything was going in slow motion in her head since she'd kissed the coin and he'd raised his hand to drop it into the machine.

Alex pulled the lever.

Penny said his name and when he turned his face to her, she kissed him; slowly and deeply as the wheels spun and spun and then, one by one they stopped.

Suddenly life zipped back to normal speed, and they were surrounded by a crowd of shouting cheering people and flashing lights and alarm bells and the sound of thousands of coins cascading down into the large bowl attached to the giant slot machine.

Penny could only stare at the rapidly growing mound of coins.

Could not believe that it was theirs and then she didn't

care because he was kissing her, on the forehead, on the cheek and finally on her mouth. And it was fine, and it was good, and she opened her mouth to him and returned his kiss with more than gentle insistence.

They stood close together as hands gave them a pat on the back and voices cheered. Penny felt his hand on her waist and the cotton of his shirt caught between her fingers and palm. Her heart was pumping, and her stomach was light and fluttery and as for the bottom half of her, well that was just pornographic.

They emerged onto the street half an hour later. A large bottle of champagne in his hand and the cheque safely stowed in his wallet.

They had barely gone twenty paces before Alex had the bottle between his thighs and was leaning over it using his thumbs to winkle the stopper out of it.

"Hey!" Penny put out a hand and nudged the bottle as his thumbs gave one more push and the cork shot out into the air followed quickly by fizzing froth.

The contents hadn't stopped gushing out of the bottle before Alex raised it to his mouth and had taken a hearty drink; and when he offered the bottle to her, Penny took it, raised it to her mouth and swallowed three, four, five mouthfuls of the fizz and foam.

"I'm so going to be sick." She laughed as she handed him the bottle.

"Me too." Alex smiled at her, drew her to him and kissed her then asked what they should do next.

"I think we should call it a night." Penny told him before she took the bottle and swallowed some more of its contents.

"Why?"

"There's nothing to do." Penny swayed a little as she looked at him and grinned.

"You spoiled my dress, took the food from my mouth,

won a shit load of money." she giggled at that "kissed me, opened the wine without breaking your nose, made me drink it and got me drunk. Err drunker." She hiccupped. "What more is there to do but go to bed."

Alex looked at her for several seconds and grinned as he took an unsteady step back and forward before taking her hand in his.

"Okay we'll go to bed."

"Good." She gave a nod of her head "let's go."

"What do you do?" Penny's head was lying on his firm chest, ten minutes later, as the lift took them up.

"Do?" he asked as his brow puckered.

"Yes, what do you do when you're not in Las Vegas?" Penny closed her eyes and breathed him in.

"I'm in London in my office making big deals and saving the world."

Penny laughed. "Really?"

Alex nodded, grinned, then shook his head.

"You don't sound like you like doing that."

"It's a family thing."

"Ahh."

"What do you do?"

Penny looked up at him for several seconds then smiled "Well I certainly don't do this!"

"What? Talk?"

Penny shook her head...

"Go out, get drunk, and eat chips." She told him as she smiled at him.

"Play the slots and win a shit load of money?" he added ...

"Exactly."

"Kiss a man, have sex!" his smile disappeared as his voice dropped to a sexy growl.

"Or that." She smiled again and he couldn't help but kiss her.

Alex dropped the Champagne bottle onto the table as they passed it on the way to her bedroom. They were lightheaded, unsteady on their feet and getting more so by the minute. He unzipped her dress and pushed it off her shoulders, kissed her at the base of her neck then tugged the hem of the dress and watched it uncover the red, lacy Basque as it dropped to the floor.

"How are you feeling C.J?" he whispered against her lips.

"I'm feeling fine Mr Sterling. Just fine." She whispered back.

"Good." He smiled as his hands went up to her neck and undid the gold chain before releasing it into his hand.

"How about we put this where it should be"

He dropped the chain onto the bed as he slid the ring onto her finger then he kissed her long and hard as his fingers swept down the hooks on the Basque and released her beautiful body into his hands.

The morning sun found her sitting on the large sofa, nursing her head, when Ashley Moore stepped out of Georgia's room. He was dishevelled and sporting overnight growth on his chin but was very nonchalant when he saw her sitting there.

"Hi Ashley."

"Hi C.J."

You lost?"

"Nope. You?"

"Not sure, puzzled really."

"About?"

"Can't say just know I am. Please tell me that Georgia isn't in there."

"Georgia isn't in there."

Penny looked at him as if she didn't believe him. Which she didn't.

"Laura." He said as he hitched a thumb at the door.

"Ahhh…" Penny sighed. "And how is Laura?"

"Quietly surprised I think."

"Hmm." Her eyes flicked to the doorway as the door opened.

"Hi Laura, you quietly surprised or lost too?"

Laura smiled as she took hold of Ashley's hand and dragged him back to the bedroom then closed the door.

"I guess neither." Penny smiled then looked at her left hand and frowned.

How had that got back onto her finger?

And how had she got back to her bedroom and undressed without being aware of doing it?

And another thing! How the hell had she woken up naked, again, and why were her female bits humming more than yesterday?

She had to take stock of herself, she decided, as she stared at the wall not really seeing the delicate flowers that covered the plaster beneath the pale wallpaper.

She must stop drinking and stay away from Alex Sterling, she told herself, because every time she was with him, she ended up like this! She gave a quick nod of her head to agree with herself then stood and headed for the bathroom.

The ring was back on the chain and suspended from her neck. Her headache was under control thanks to pills and a visit to the toilet and she was among the girls again, on their way to the shops at the other end of the town.

The shop lights weren't so stark and bright in the sunshine she noticed, and the streets were not so threatening as they were at night, which was reassuring.

Penny glanced down an alley as they walked past it and felt a slight pull as if it were calling to her to return there. She frowned, as her feet faltered, and then she found she had to skip to catch up with the others.

"You're sure we haven't been here before?" she asked Georgia as she turned her head towards the alley that was now several feet behind them.

"Pretty much, we shopped at the other end of town yesterday don't you remember?"

Penny nodded as she caught sight of the giant slot machine twenty feet in front of her and stopped walking as a memory slipped into her head and sped out again.

"You okay C.J? You look like you've seen a ghost."

"I'm okay Georgie, just thinking I'll stay in my room tonight is all."

"You can't do that! You promised you'd join in, no excuses."

"I'm not going to survive this at all." Penny groaned as Georgia took her arm and led her towards a duo of shops whose windows extolled a great shopping experience.

"Great experience my eye." Penny murmured under her breath as they stepped out of the shop and back into the sunshine.

"Rather be naked than wearing that in my bed."

"Shut up".

The quietly whispered command was directed at the voice in her head that had snorted at her choice of words because she didn't need any reminders of her nakedness, thanks very much.

The voice took heed and left her in peace as she stepped into line with the other women, and they progressed down the row of female orientated shops.

~

The guys were at a loose end. They'd already shot holes in the desert and played the slots till they were nearly bankrupt now what could they do to relieve the boredom.

They could go to a pub, or rather, go on a bar crawl but, if they got drunk early in the day, they wouldn't be in a fit state to chaperone the girls when they all partied that night; and party they must, because it was their last night there.

What they needed now, right this second, they decided, was to meet up with the girls because they were pretty good at dreaming up something to do, and it wouldn't hurt to spend the day with them again; because, let's face it, they'd spent all the previous ones in their company anyway.

"Laura said they'd be in the west end today." Ashley said, around the plastic straw in his mouth.

"The west end?" Bertie asked.

"Yeah, they're going shopping."

"Shall we go meet them?" Bertie Hicks tried not to sound too excited by the idea, but it was getting harder to hide his enthusiasm when the prospect of seeing Millie was in the offing.

"We could head that way." Rob said.

Alex decided he was losing his head and not just because of the painful hangovers he'd been self-inflicting on himself.

"Have we done the slots up there?" he asked as the sun shone into his eyes "I'm losing my sense of direction, but I could swear we have."

"Nope, not one of them and can honestly say I'm not interested."

"YEAH!" came a chorus from Ashley and Bertie.

"Hey!" Alex called out as they closed in on the girls a few minutes later.

"Hey" Penny's voice lacked enthusiasm.

"You, okay?" Alex made his way to her and just stopped himself from reaching for her hand.

"Just a little bit puzzled and a lot hung over."

Penny didn't smile, didn't really look at him either.

"You?"

"Same." He said as he gave her a quick smile.

"I'm not going out tonight," she told him "I'm staying in my room, going to sketch some ideas I have and sip on iced tea." She sighed and gave a small nod of her head as if doing so would make it happen.

"Don't think that's allowed." Alex told her, but his tone said he didn't want to go out tonight either.

"Yeah, well, my stomach can't stand another drop of alcohol, nor can my head."

"And not being able to remember stuff is kind of scary." He offered.

"Yeah, no memory, that's the worst thing, I mean how come I wake up star... err in the morning with no memory of how I got back to my room?"

(Or why my body is purring like a contented kitten and my lips are red and numb.)

She felt the blood invade her face at the thought and turned away from him.

"Hey Alex Sterling! Are you talking dirty to C.J?"

Rob looked about ready to hang him.

"No Rob I'm not talking dirty to C.J. nor would I for God's sake."

"She not your type?" Bertie Hicks was smiling at him; he obviously didn't value his teeth.

"No, she's not my type." Alex said, in lieu of bopping Bertie in the mouth.

"Okay, let's move on shall we." Laura was getting bored. "You guys going somewhere special?"

"Nope." All the male heads were shaking no, but Penny decided they could just all go to hell, with Alex Sterling at the head of the line.

(And they should take Laura with them.)

They didn't go back to the hotel, or to the slots. They just walked around the town talking and laughing and before she knew it Penny had unknowingly shown that she was well versed on a lot of topics, and she'd managed to stay away from anything woody or wood related (because no-one needed to know that she was overly knowledgeable on trees and wood processes or the finer qualities of metal and precious gems.)

At seven thirty, after they'd all dined on yet more fast food, and their camaraderie was at its height, Penny dipped down to pick up her bag and the ring dropped out from under the neckline of her shirt.

It was like the end of the world was imminent and she, according to Alex Sterling, was the person who had pushed the button, lit the fuse, plunged the plunger.

Oh, and she was also a thief and a bastard, a thieving bastard, because the ring hanging on that chain was his and she'd obviously nicked it when he was in his cups.

Was he serious?

No one called being drunk 'in their cups' anymore and she'd found the damn ring on her finger, twice. She told him that too, but he'd snorted like a rampaging bull as he'd all but wrenched the thing from her neck.

"Did you nick it C.J.?" Bertie Hicks grinned at her as he wiggled his unruly eyebrows.

"No Bertie, I didn't nick it, but I can bust your lip if you like." She smiled sweetly at him, and he beat a hasty retreat back to Millie.

"Penny?" Georgia whispered.

"No, I didn't Georgia, I found it. That's it! I don't want to talk any more, don't need to be friends with any of you at the moment; what I do want, and need, is a drink, a big strong alcohol filled glass of anything; and if it makes me sick, I'm going to make sure I aim for his god dammed big feet, and see how he likes it."

"Likes what C.J.?"

"Don't know, don't care. Now where's the nearest bar?" Penny let her eyes run along the length of the street then set off in the direction of the closest set of winking lights.

"I'm going back to the hotel."

It was half past nine and Penny squinted as she spoke to Georgia.

"And I'm gonna put my jammies on tonight, waste of time bringing them if I don't at least wear them once."

"You been sleeping naked Pen? You never sleep naked."

"I know." Penny grinned "but I'm wearing them tonight because I don't want to wake up feeling like that again."

"Like what? Penny?" Georgia put a hand on Penny's arm and frowned at her. "Penny?"

Penny shrugged, gave Georgia a fragile look then raised a glass to her mouth and took a long, long drink.

"Take her back to her room and make sure she goes inside."

Rob ignored the protest that flew at him from Georgia's mouth as he stared into Alex's eyes; but he wasn't sure Alex was listening.

"You hear me? Alex!"

Alex nodded.

'Take her back to her room and go inside.'

The words kept running through his brain as he escorted C.J back to the hotel. She was walking very nicely in her bare feet, his eyes travelled up to her backside, it was moving nicely too.

"I need a drink." Penny didn't look at him.

"O-kay." He agreed.

"And some chips." She added quickly.

"Chips sounds good too."

"Okay?"

"Okay."

"How did you get that?" Penny pointed to the scar above

Alex's left elbow as he raised a chip filled hand towards his face.

"Broke it." He mumbled as he shoved several chips into his mouth.

"Me too." She showed him her right elbow as she smiled at him.

"I fell out of a tree and suffered for it." He told her.

"I had an accident with a tree too."

Alex watched as a trio of chips slowly disappeared between her lips and resisted the urge to take a share.

"What happened, you fall against it and break a nail?" Alex grinned.

"No." she grinned back, but I once fell over a root and broke a finger."

"Really?" Alex jerked his lips down in a quick sympathetic grimace then allowed them to go back up.

"Yes, but that wasn't the accident." Penny continued.

"It wasn't?" Alex frowned.

"No. When I was ten, I was climbing this big oak tree in my dads' back garden. It was really tall, and its branches spread out for yards and yards. It was really easy to climb up but coming down was harder."

"Why did you climb up it?"

"To bring Harry down."

"Who is Harry?"

"Harry was my cat; he was big and black and stupid."

"So why did you want to save him?"

"He was my cat, and he was stuck up the tree." Why else her frown told him.

"Couldn't your dad get him down?"

"Mum and Dad were in America."

"So, you went up the tree and what happened?"

"I got hold of the cat, tucked him into my shirt and started to climb down. Three branches to go and he squirmed, got out of my shirt and was on the ground in seconds. I was knocked off balance and I fell. It was really weird though because, as I fell, I swear, a branch moved and broke my fall." She looked at him with serious eyes. "But it was really the wind, I think."

"And you were, okay?"

"Yes. Well. No actually."

Alex waited and several seconds later she told him.

"So, the branch moved as I fell, and I dropped onto it and then I rolled off and kind of floated to the ground." She grinned, "No..." she held up a hand..." I fell to the ground." She confessed.

"Was it very high?"

She looked at him. Ran her eyes down his torso and over his bent knees to his feet. "Taller than you." She told him as his groin tingled and his trousers tightened.

"So over six feet."

"You aren't six feet tall Alex Sterling!"

"I'm not?"

"Nope. Five feet nine or ten."

"So higher than five feet nine or ten inches then."

"Yeah, it was like, twelve feet."

"You sure?"

She gave him a quick look then smiled "no it was fifteen feet, straight down."

"Good to know you weren't hurt."

"Oh, I got hurt. The tree saved my life, but I had to pay for it."

She was rubbing her elbow as a small pucker appeared between her eyes.

"The tree caught my side, cut it open for inches and stabbed me on the side of my neck, and when I hit the ground, I broke my arm."

"Christ!"

"No. Oak. I've loved that tree ever since. Dad wanted to chop it down, but I told him it wasn't the trees fault."

"Very magnanimous of you."

She looked at him. Flicked her eyes across his face and held his eyes for a second or two.

"It's given me lots of material and allows me to produce beautiful things, so I don't see it that way."

"It's only a tree."

"You should come see it sometime, it's the most amazing thing I know."

The conversation ended when he ordered another beer and they shared it as they walked along the street.

Another stop in a bar, another drink and they were holding on to each other as they walked along the pavement towards their hotel, because they were pretty much drunk. (Okay they were really drunk.).

"Time for bed."

Penny smiled at him as they entered the hotel and made for the bank of elevators.

Alex didn't argue.

4

TAKE ME HOME SILVER BIRD AND
AWAY FROM THE INSANITY

Alex woke up, lying on top of his bed, his shirt was hanging off his shoulders and his trousers were open.

His head was also banging, and his eyes were stinging. He'd been having a good dream, a nice dream. He closed his eyes and tried to conjure it up again, but it had melted away; so, he lay still and thought about the vision instead; but nothing was clear to him except a long silver line that had marred the soft white skin his lips had gently explored.

He groaned. He was going round the bend; too much alcohol and bright lights were making him soft and stupid. When he got home, he decided, he was going to go tee total, leave his libido in his bedroom, alone, and just regroup.

What could go wrong?

Penny was in pain, and was more than a little puzzled. Her nether regions were humming again, and her head was pounding.

Roll on England and sanity.

She got up, went into the bathroom, showered, and brushed her teeth then sat on her bed twiddling the ring between her fingers. It had appeared again; out of the blue and she didn't know what to do with it because, if she tried to give it back to Alex, he'd have her arrested for theft. So, after a couple of minutes of contemplation, she stood up and tossed it onto the clothes in her suitcase before grabbing her bag and leaving the room.

It was their last day; eviction from their hotel room was at twelve, a time bartered for before they booked. After that there would be a five-hour wait before the plane took off and they'd finally be heading back to civilised living.

No bright lights, no booze, no sex, no hangovers.

'Bring it on.'

~

They'd been on the flight for two hours when Laura disappeared, Penny was sleeping, and Millie was listening to something on the headphones when Bertie appeared and motioned her to follow him. A second later Rob dropped into the seat next to Georgia and Alex took the one next to Penny.

"She's out of it." Alex gave a quick look in Penny's direction and saw Georgia nod.

"She's all in. Not surprising though, she doesn't do this a lot. Not at all really."

"Fly in an aeroplane?" asked Alex.

"Or party 'n' drink" Georgia told him

"Or have a hangover." Rob smiled. "And puke up."

"Then why did she come?"

"Because she's my maid of honour and my best friend."

"So... what's her name? What does C.J. stand for?"

"I don't like that name!" Georgia was frowning and her eyes had become a little angry. "Someone gave it to her a long time ago and it follows her around like a bad smell."

She gave Rob a quick look, saw him shake his head then returned her eyes to Alex.

"We can't tell you. It was part of the deal. Signed in blood and under threat of death." She grinned at his sudden frown. "Only joking about the blood, but the death threat is true so I truly can't tell you."

Alex gave a nod of understanding then leaned back in the seat.

"She gets angry when something happens to her."

His chin went up in the direction of Penny, but his eyes stayed on Georgia and Rob.

"Don't we all?" Robs' eyes hardened as he looked at his friend.

"Yeah, I guess, but she goes off in search of blood."

"When someone makes her live up to that name, yes she does and before you ask, I can't tell you." Georgia's eyes were as hard as her fiancés.

"Then I'll ask her when she wakes up."

"You can do that Alex." Rob had his poker face on "but she won't tell you, she doesn't like you, you called her a thieving bastard, and she won't forgive you for that."

"She had my ring. How did she get it if she didn't take it?"

"I have no idea, maybe you dropped it and she found it, maybe you gave it to her and don't remember, maybe you shouldn't accuse her of anything till you know her and the facts, because, Alex, she's not a thief; anyone who *really* knows her, knows that as fact."

Penny had had a long glass of fizzy water with a dash of lime an hour ago, now she needed the loo. The one nearest to her chair was occupied and had been for the past fifteen minutes, there was nothing for it, she'd have to use the one near big foot with the pointy elbows. She sighed as she got up, smiled at Georgia and set off.

She was back in her seat within ten minutes because there

had been no obstacles in her way to impede her journey. She almost wished there had been.

"You okay Penny?" Georgia smiled but her eyes held a small amount of concern.

"Yes, just thinking a nice curry would go down well."

"Hmm. How about we book one for Wednesday night. Have it delivered while we watch a movie?"

"Yeah. that would be nice, but no alcohol." Penny said.

"Ok no alcohol." Georgia nodded.

5

WEDDING MINUS THREE DAYS

Three weeks after they had returned home a letter arrived in Penny's post; it looked very official and important lying there on her desk. Penny took a quick sip of her coffee then set the cup down, flicked the envelope over and over between her fingers and finally opened it.

She read it.

Then read it again.

The cover note was brief and to the point, but she didn't understand why it had been sent to her; so, she moved on to the several sheets of paper that had bright pink pointers indicating where she had to sign and she frowned; what did they think she was, for God's sake, a bloody idiot?

"What do you mean you have to sign some divorce papers? You aren't married! Are you?" Georgia was looking at her like she should be locked up and the key thrown away.

"Not that I know, and I should because I would be the one who said yes."

"Is there a name on the papers stating who the groom is, err, was?"

Penny ran her eyes over the short letter. "Nope. Just says client. My client has instructed me..."

"Let me see." Georgia held out her hand then shook it impatiently when the papers weren't put into it quick enough.

"Did you meet a hobo on the street and take pity on him?" Georgia asked Penny several minutes later.

Penny almost laughed.

"No Georgia I didn't meet a hobo and marry him."

"Good. No hobo. What about a busker, did you see a busker?"

This was starting to sound ridiculous. Yes, she took pity on homeless people sitting on the street and always dropped a fiver into a buskers' collection bowl, but she wasn't about to marry one.

"I was with you all the time Georgia!"

"Did you take a stranger to our hotel room Penny?"

"No, I did not, and it wasn't ours it was mine and Laura's and Ashley's actually."

Georgia had the good grace to go pink.

"So, what are you going to do?"

Penny sighed. "Well first I'm going to get my name changed to C.J. I've involved myself in the calamity of the year with this so I might as well."

"You are not a Clumsy Jane Penny Craig."

"Yeah, well, I look better now all the bruises are gone, but my eyebrow has a spot where there is no hair, and I don't think it will ever grow back. Bloody big foot and his damn big feet."

"We've been home three weeks Pen. How many accidents have you had huh?"

"None I guess."

"Right! So! No Clumsy Jane. Now, what about the letter?"

"Sign it and send it back, I guess. Could be a saving grace, he might be a midget or look like a Neanderthal."

"He could also be six foot six and a hunk."

"Shall I forget it then?"

"You could wait and see what happens or call up the solicitor and ask to meet."

Penny was shaking her head. Meeting the solicitor was the last thing she wanted, and anyway her time was pretty much taken up with air flights and meeting clients for the next week at least. So, mister Neanderthal would have to wait (and she, for one, could withstand the suspense.)

By the time Penny got back, a week later, the letter was still on her desk but hidden under several packages, notes and an array of metal cut outs with different coloured tags on them.

It was Friday. The Friday before Rob's wedding. The wedding party were already assembled for the service practice at five after which would be a pre wedding dinner at their mothers' home, followed by drinks.

Penny had barely set foot in the door, suitcase in hand, before her arm was taken and she was rushed up to her room.

"Georgia, please I'm pooped!"

"You have five minutes then we're leaving. Be quick."

"I need longer than that."

"Tough! Five minutes, you shower I'll get you something to wear."

"Okay. But nothing sexy ay?" She called as she headed for her bathroom.

"Nothing sexy... O...Kay." Mouthed Georgia as she stepped up to the wardrobe with a smile on her face; because everything Penny wore was sexy, even her scruffy boots and baggy jeans. She ran her hands over the sparse number of dresses that hung in the closet, found what she was looking for and dropped it onto the bed; thought about adding the red Basque then ignored it.

"Is he here?" Penny asked as she stepped into her dress.

"He?"

"Alex Sterling."

"He's part of the wedding group so, yes, he's here. Why?"

"Just need to know if I should put on some armour, or a boxer's helmet and some steel toed boots."

"You *are* tired. Bed for you by midnight Cinderella."

"Yeah. " Penny agreed on a sigh as she started to pull the dress up her body.

Seven minutes later she opened her bedroom door and turned to Georgia as she stepped through it.

"Can you tell them to just call me Penny?... I'm tired of being C.J. it's not me anymore."

"Ok Pen, I'll tell them, and if they don't listen to me, I'll get Rob to have a go at them."

Georgia smiled "You were never a Clumsy Jane in the first place Pen. Bloody Laura and her mouth should be banned from holding a conversation, EVER."

Penny grinned then kissed Georgia on the cheek because suddenly she felt a lot better.

～

Penny ignored Alex everywhere.

At the church.

At the dinner table.

At every opportunity.

But it was harder to do it when they were all assembled in the lounge and throughout the bottom of the house.

She didn't drink, well not a lot, a toast here and there were of little consequence, or should have been only she was jet lagged and tired, so, as the night got longer her temper got shorter.

"You drunk?" asked Alex Sterling quite suddenly from beside her.

Penny squinted at him. "No, I'm not drunk."

"You hungry?"

"I've just eaten the equivalent of one cow and a farm load of veg so, no, I'm not hungry."

"Can I get you a drink?"

She sighed and walked away from him; and kept going, into the kitchen, where she picked up a torch, then out into the garden and the night, where Tree stood proud and strong.

"Hi" She whispered as she ran her hand over the deeply veined bark.

"I'm back."

She wrapped her arms around the trunk and laid her cheek against it.

"I've finished them and the charms. They'll love them, I think. Thank you."

A branch above her creaked and she smiled.

"Is this your tree?"

"God" she thought before she answered,

"Not mine but my tree yes."

(Didn't that mean the same thing?) Alex frowned.

"What do you want Mister Sterling?"

She didn't look at him as she tried not to let his being there affect her at all.

"Just making sure you're okay." He told her as his eyes remained on her face.

"And why would you do that?"

"You're my responsibility, remember, we all have a responsibility to one of the bridesmaids, you, unfortunately, are mine."

"I relieve you of the inconvenience, so you can go."

"You want a drink?"

"No..." she said on a long sigh.

"I do not want a drink. I've just about pickled my liver and abused my head till it's permanently dizzy, so take it away."

"It's good stuff. Expensive Brut."

"You can take your brew and.." the branch above her creaked again and she looked up at it. The leaves rustled and a couple fell. Penny frowned and shook her head. Several more leaves fell to the ground, so she whispered *'okay'* and turned to him.

"I'll have a drink if you climb up."

"Up."

"Yes, I've been told to invite you and, despite my thinking better of it, I 'm doing it. I'm inviting you up."

"It's dark."

"Are you scared?"

"No but it's dark!"

"So, you've said. But I have a light, so you'll be quite safe."

Penny swung the lantern to the front of her then flicked her finger over the switch and the camping light glowed. Then she hooked it onto a small sturdy twig before she kicked off her shoes.

Her lovely legs disappeared up into the tree and a few seconds later the branch above him dipped then settled back in position.

'I knew he wouldn't do it'

He heard her whisper as his foot settled onto a thick branch.

'All talk and no...'

"Hi."

Alex smiled at her as he stuck his head into the small canvas structure that looked a bit unsteady, suspended as it was, between the upper large branch and the thinner lower one.

"Sit down before you fall off." She told him, firmly.

"Okay."

He sat.

"You want a drink now?" he asked as he produced a bottle from inside his shirt.

(Creak)

"Yes. Yes, I'll have a damn drink." She huffed at him.

"Good."

Alex smiled as he popped the cork from the bottle then handed the bottle to her.

"So" he kind of sighed as a precursor to what he wanted to say.

"Don't talk Alex, just lie still and breathe." Penny said quickly

"I breathe all the time, it's a necessity if I want to live."

"Well, another necessity is not talking."

"At all?"

"For ten minutes. No talking for ten minutes, only lying here quietly."

"And drinking." He added, a second before he took a few mouthfuls of the liquid then held the bottle out to her again.

The tree creaked and she took it.

Half an hour later the bottle was nearly empty, and Penny was giggling.

"Is this the tree you fell out of?" Alex asked her.

"Yes."

"Me too."

"No!" she sat up straight and the tent like structure wobbled.

"Yeah, I'd come round to see Rob, we were going to go out on some buggies but I kind of put an end to that when I fell out of the tree.

"Why did you climb it?"

He shrugged. "Just did."

"No cat?"

"Nope."

The branches creaked and Penny swallowed down the final mouthful of liquid.

"Bottle's empty." She told him as she held it out to him.

"That's not a problem, I have another down below."

"Another one?" Penny groaned. "I don't think I can drink anymore."

"Shall we try?"

"I'll pass but you can drink as much as you like if you walk me home."

"Home?"

"To the house."

"Okay." Alex took a deep breath "But we need to get down first."

Alex felt Penny move next to him, felt the pressure of her hand on his knee and then she was gone. When he poked his head out of the tent, he was surprised to see her standing among the leaves, as if waiting for him.

"It's dark, so it's best you follow me, okay?" she told him.

Alex didn't move anything but his eyes. They flicked several times towards the ground and back to where Penny was standing, rather confidently, amongst the leaves and branches.

Penny waited five seconds for him to follow her out of the tent before she sat on the thinning branches beneath her feet, then nudged her bottom forward and dropped off them.

Alex felt his heart hit his boots then he panicked and moved to the edge of the branches without much care, and once there he launched himself off and down towards the ground. No mean feat considering he didn't know how far away the ground was because any light visible from below was negated by the branches and the dark surrounding him.

His knees buckled when he landed, and his breath was forced out as a pained "oof."

"You, okay?" Penny tucked her hand under his arm and tried to pick him up. Which was somewhat awkward as he was trying his best to make her release him.

"You came down a bit quick." Alex grumbled.

Penny grinned and he frowned at her.

"You have to move forward until the branches bend then go with them." She told him as if it were a well-known fact.

"I thought you'd fallen off and broken your stupid neck." Alex grumbled again.

"Nope just slid off there like jelly off a plate." Penny told him as she stood up, collected her shoes, and then put some space between them.

"Head still on shoulders and neck in one piece. Goodnight grouch."

Penny turned and walked off, hoping he would take the hint and stay away from her. But he caught up with her in what felt like half a second.

"You want a drink?" he asked her again.

Penny stopped walking as she battered down the instinct to tell him where he could shove the bottle, but then she gave a nod of her head instead.

Alex raised the bottle to her lips and held it as she sipped the contents.

He could see her throat move as she swallowed and smell the sweet perfume of her shower gel; and when her tongue started to lick the fizzy alcohol from her lips, he felt his groin tighten painfully before he brought his mouth down onto hers.

She was delicious he thought as his lips and tongue moved over hers.

She was in love, she thought, as she clung to him in the dark.

"You hungry?" he asked against her lips a few seconds later.

Penny shook her head.

"Thirsty?"

"No."

Penny hesitated then smiled as her mind clouded over in a tipsy drunken veil.

"I think it's time for bed." She whispered as his mouth closed over hers.

'Oh, Dear God!'

Penny dropped the covers over her naked body and swallowed hard against the lump in her throat. Her head was banging. Her stomach was swimming, and her nightclothes were still on the chair, folded and clean.

Dare she look at her finger? Dare she?

He opened his eyes. It was painful. His head was banging, his stomach was a little unsteady and his memory was pretty much absent. He was hung over and it was activity day. He closed his eyes for several minutes, rubbed his palm across his forehead and then tried to construct an absence note in his head.

An absence note. Was that the best he could come up with?

Was he a child?

Well... No, he wasn't BUT he WAS trying to get out of doing some exercise because he needed to stay where he was until he felt more human.

More able to cope.

With C.J.

With his feelings.

With C.J.

'SHIT!'

"Penny! Penny you, okay?"

Georgia was frowning at her; she seemed to do a lot of that recently.

"No." Penny groaned as she looked at her breakfast plate.

"Are you hanging over?"

"Yeah... And under I think..."

"Thought you weren't going to drink."

"So did I?"

"You going to be, okay?"

"Yeah." Penny gave a weak smile then headed out to the bathroom.

Painkillers were a wonderful invention, so was toast and coffee. All three had been forced down and within an hour Penny was feeling more human.

But Alex had thrown the gauntlet down to his stomach and had eaten his way through a cooked breakfast, with two cups of coffee and a couple of rounds of toast.

He felt great. Just had to get through the weekend, do his best man stuff on Monday, make the speeches and toasts and then he could head home.

What could go wrong?

Penny smiled at her mother as she made her way down to her workrooms. She'd been away on business a bit longer than she had wanted to be which wasn't good as she had to make some final alterations to one of her pieces and check on her mail.

The alterations took a little over an hour and forty-five minutes. When they were complete, she brought out a silver cloth and gave all the pieces assembled on the worktop a final shine before putting them into their designated boxes. When they were lined up on the countertop, in two straight rows, Penny dropped her eyes onto the pile of mail and stuff on the edge of her desk and sighed as she picked it up.

The metal and tags could wait she decided as she sat in her chair.

The brown packages were a mix of immediate and not so important stuff and the letters could all be answered on Tuesday, when the wedding was over, and the house was quiet again.

And then there was the light cream envelope.

Her eyes flicked across its surface as her mouth dipped.

It still looked important and dangerous.

She opened it, unfolded the several pieces of paper and reread it.

She should really sign it.

Send it back from whence it came.

Put an end to the whole sorry business.

But she couldn't. She didn't know why; she just knew she couldn't.

So, she opened a drawer and dropped the letter inside.

6

WEDDING MINUS TWO DAYS

"You can't stay in here Penny! We have things to do."

Georgia stuck her head through the door to Penny's office and heard Penny groan.

"You promised you'd be good." Georgia smiled at her.

"Yeah, well, how many times have I broken that vow?"

"Are you okay?"

"Not really I've been feeling a little off lately and I woke up naked again!"

"Really? When you were away?"

"No Georgia, not when I was away, I don't make a habit of waking up starkers in strange hotel rooms."

"Here then?"

"Yes here!"

A few strands of Penny's unruly hair drifted forward as she blew out a sigh.

"Aww I do feel rough." She admitted.

"That'll be the booze." Georgia grinned.

"Yeah, well, next time he offers it to me I'm going to refuse it."

"He?"

"Big foot. All he ever does is ply me with drink and food,

bloody beer and chips and then some special brew. My stomach is still at sea from Vegas, and I go and do it again."

"Do what, exactly?"

"Get drunk and wake up naked."

"And feel sick?"

"Yeah." Penny gave her a smile. "It's good you came here though Georgia."

"To the house?"

"To my studio, I have something for you."

Penny moved one row of the small boxes to the centre of her desk then muddled them up.

"Choose a box, any box."

Georgia tapped a finger on a box then picked it up when Penny dipped her head as a sign of permission.

Inside the dark blue cube sat a pair of cuff links. The gold winked at Georgia as she took one out and ran a thumb over the smooth wooden totem that sat in the middle of the 18 carat gold setting.

"Those ones are for Rob. Thought you'd like a reminder of your stay in Vegas, so I made a copy of the totem in the sand, where we ate the hot dogs and Millie put her gender rumours to bed. The groomsmen have the same."

She opened another box

"Only theirs are made in silver."

"Penny."

"And these are for the girls."

Penny opened two boxes. Inside of which, sitting on the white satin cloth, were perfect replicas of the totems, set in silver or gold and suspended from a thin corded neck chain that moved slightly when picked up.

"Yours is in gold, the girls in silver."

"Penny I..."

"I thought you'd maybe want something to give to them, but if you already have something then no worries."

"No, no"

Georgia's eyes began to fill with tears

"I love them, all of them." She whispered.

"Good, then take them away, but not this one it's mine."

Penny tapped the top of one of the boxes then grinned.

"Only kidding." She said as she raised her hand off the box before turning her attention back on Georgia and asking her if she knew where Rob was.

That evening Alex had a few minutes to kill before going downstairs. They were all going out on the town. In relation to London, it was a small place to go out on, and probably didn't have anything to keep them occupied for longer than an hour or so. But out he'd go because he was best man and the best man's job was to keep an eye on the groom.

He took out his phone and speed dialled his solicitor. Apologised to him for phoning him on a Saturday evening but he needed to know if there was any progress with the annulment. It had, after all, been four weeks since he'd asked him to get it done and he'd heard nothing.

"So, how's it going? ... Not signed, why not? ... Have you met with her? ... Okay has she been in contact at all... Not for anything?"

"You can keep hold of your wallet Alex. She won't be asking for money."

Mike Ford tried to calm his friend but knew it wasn't working.

"I checked out your hotel in Vegas, a Penelope Craig was registered there the same time you stayed. I did a background check, she's English, lives with her mother and is by no means poor."

"And you know this because?"

"She's Penelope Craig."

"And?"

"You don't know who Penelope Craig is?"

"She's my soon to be ex-wife that's all I need to know."

"I could send out another letter. Word it a bit stronger. You need her to sign because?"

"Because I want out. I'm not paying her a penny for the privilege either."

"This girl doesn't need your cash, Alex."

"Word it how you like, just get it done.' He hung up, looked at his watch and went downstairs.

For a small town it wasn't so bad. The centre was only minutes away from the house, so they'd all got there in cabs. No cars to drive back, no rules about drinking to worry about and no licences to lose.

The streets were still visible in the natural light of dusk and although the lights were out behind most of the shop windows several were illuminating the pavements and air with a yellow or red glow.

"My round!" Rob shouted into the din coating the bar area. "C.J.?"

"Cola, please." She told him and a second later she took the glass from him and sipped at the dark liquid.

When Rob felt a tug on his jacket, he turned round and found himself looking into his sisters' eyes.

"I said cola Rob not whatever this is."

"Lighten up Pen." He told her quietly, "One drink won't hurt."

Then he grinned at her before turning away.

Penny placed the glass onto the counter and didn't touch it again.

"You haven't touched your drink."

Georgia pointed at the full glass as she came to a stop next to Penny.

"It's not like you're going to need it though... sign over the bar says Karaoke is cancelled again...Shame..."

"Me too..." inserted Millie "I think there's a conspiracy..."

79

"REALLY!" chorused Georgia and Penny.

"Yeah..." Millie gave them a tipsy-ish look then left them.

"From America..." said a voice into the air... ".... Fluffy Flamingooo..."

The room erupted as 'The Fluffy Flamingo" walked out in front of the crowd...

Penny raised her glass as she turned to take a look at the small stage and there she was, the same queen that had interrupted the karaoke in Vegas. Only this time her pink wig removed all the hair from her face and swept it up into a high Ponytail that sat on top of her head and, once again, woven into the hair were the soft baby feathers that exaggerated the ponytail while adding a duck down softness to the rest of the hair.

She was dressed exquisitely in a pink bodice covered with varying lengths of soft feathers in shades of pink, from cerise to baby. Her eyes were as big as before, her legs were encased in shining baby pink-coloured stockings and on her feet were boots in that oh so soft leather, only this time they were a pale orange that matched the lipstick she'd applied to her nicely shaped lips.

She looked stunning... and, Penny thought... somehow... very familiar, like they'd met up close and personal...

Penny frowned as her hand moved the glass towards her mouth; her fingers wrapped tight around the frosted, wet surface as she took a mouthful of liquid.

"Drink up and I'll get you another. What is it?" Georgia asked as she caught the bar-mans' attention.

"Rum and cola." Penny said as she released the glass.

"And now there are two'" She thought as a second glass was placed next to the first.

Penny had finished the first drink and had moved onto the second glass when she began to feel a little uncomfortable, like someone was looking at her... no... like someone was watching her every move, which was a bit unusual because she'd pretty much ignored the Flamingo in favour of doing a memory search of that same bird.

But nothing came to her... Nothing... Except the cuts and bruises... and the shots... and the fact that she'd woken up in her bed as naked as naked could be...

But then... *"Shit... shit...shi..."*

Penny whispered as she saw herself being pulled towards a flashing light and an open door.

The vision continued in a mixed-up unintelligible mess until Penny heard herself say "I do" and felt a ring being slipped onto her finger but, when she looked up to see who had put it there the face was fuzzy and out of focus, like she was looking through the eyes of someone who was drunk.

Oh... Dear.... God!...

Penny ran a hand through her hair then picked up her glass and tried to erase the truth by taking a large mouthful of its intoxicating contents; but it didn't work, the truth ran round in her head wearing a glittery tiara and body-hugging dress...and then there were the small sexually posed figures.

Penny blinked several times because there was no getting away from it, she'd gone into a wedding parlour in Vegas, with a complete stranger and said I do when a man dressed as... she frowned... dressed as a... (deep swallow) ...woman...asked her if she did.

What on earth had possessed her to do that?

"Several alcoholic beverages, three shots, two beers, a few chips and some very, very soft lips." Came the answer.

The memory slipped back into the cave in her brain from which it had surfaced and in doing so it brought the letter to mind, she could see it sitting in her desk drawer and the sight of it made her wince. Maybe it would be better to sign it, slide it into the return envelope and just slip away into obscurity as it made its merry way back to where it came from.

That would be the best thing to do.

Don't go see the lawyer. Don't go see or contact the groom; just slide away into obscurity.

Okay?

Okay!

Forty minutes and three drinks later, Fluffy was still entertaining the crowd with her jokes and chatter, so Penny decided to get closer to her...

"Hello..." said the deep voice of the Flamingo... "So nice to see you again..."

(Uh Oh...)

"You look extra lovely tonight..." carried on the voice. "Unlike a certain someone who just can't help being...."

"I love your outfit..." Penny offered quickly.

"Isn't it gorgeous..." Fluffy ran the tips of her fingers over the feathers that graced the front of her body....

"Yes... it is..." whispered Penny... "It must take a long time to make... I mean sooo many feathers..." Penny's eyes swept up and down the tall female... "and I just love the diamonds on your eyes and lashes..."

"It's Dusti's work... you remember Dusti, she's just so clever... she has some gorgeous jewellery... and she can get anyone to agree to anything..."

Penny was shaking her head; she didn't know anyone called Dusti...not at all... but she did, kind of, remember being very close to a beehive and a very, very, delightful tiara...

∾

Penny's eyes were caught and held by Alex's as she was finishing her, third or fourth drink before she stepped outside for some air. Her mind was too mixed up and fuzzy to remain inside any longer and, in truth, she didn't want to be around Fluffy anymore, because that woman knew something, and it would only take a second for that something to be general knowledge should Fluffy decide to open her beak and let it out.

Drink imbibed... Penny went outside.

"Are you hungry." Alex asked from behind her a mere minute later.

Penny sighed a tired *"Nope."*

"Want a drink?"

(Oh Lord! Déjà vu was not a kind or friendly thing.)

"I've had my quota." She took a deep frustrated breath and pushed it back out.

"Chippies open, want some?"

"That's food, I'm not hungry."

Alex bought some chips and she helped herself to some, putting them into her mouth as they walked along the darkened street.

"Do you want a hand with them?" he asked her softly, almost lovingly, when they stopped for a moment, and she swayed a little to the front and back.

"Them?" Penny asked around the duo of chunky chips that were poking out of her mouth like two slim cigars waiting for a light.

Alex didn't answer; he just leaned forward and nibbled away at the chips until his lips touched hers; and he was quietly surprised when she didn't complain (this time).

Penny, on the other hand, wished her mouth wasn't full of potato, because if it hadn't been she'd have kissed him back, long and hard.

Alex, unaware of her thoughts, finished the last of the chips and tugged her into a small bar; where they drank a beer between them, slugged back a couple of shots and felt the world disappear into a face tingling fog.

7

WEDDING MINUS ONE DAY

The next morning, Penny woke up naked, her head was banging, her feminine bits were humming and, on her left ring finger, sat the old ring that belonged to Alex.

"You feel alright Penny?" Georgia asked as she settled into her chair at breakfast. "You looked fit to bust last night; Rob sent Alex after you when you left the pub; just to make sure you were okay." Georgia was looking at her as if she had a fragile sign hanging round her neck.

And as she WAS, in fact, feeling very fragile, she said, "I think I'll stay here today."

"It's going to be a lovely day Penny, so we decided to go to the abbey grounds. Come too, ay? You like it there."

"But its miles away Georgie, and I don't feel too good."

"You'll be fine. Come on!"

Penny slid into the back of the car and found herself sitting next to Alex. He was pale and distant. She didn't mind, talking was the last thing she wanted to do; so, she dropped her head onto the back of the seat and, within a few minutes, had fallen asleep. Alex didn't complain when her head fell onto his shoulder. But then he didn't really know it was there because his mind was working overtime; sifting through his memories and putting them into boxes as he searched for the one memory that still eluded him.

Penny had been sitting in her favourite place, under a trio of trees whose branches intertwined above her head as their leaves rustled in the slight breeze.

It was a lovely, quiet, perhaps romantic place to be.

Until Georgia sat down beside her and gave her arm a tug.

"Are you feeling better?"

Penny nodded.

"Want to go to the island? The little café has coffee and tea and snacks. And you can sit on a chair instead of the ground."

Penny went. It was easier to agree than not and she *was* feeling a little peckish.

At the café everyone ordered tea and chips, and burgers except Penny who had a bottle of water and a salad roll.

She felt better after eating and stepped away, camera in hand, to take some photos of the wooded area next to the building. She had just focused her lens on a very pretty looking tree whose bark was gnarled and pitted with deep veins and was about to press the shutter release when someone stepped into the shot. The carefully crafted photo quickly blurred and went out of focus and then, because Penny's finger was way past the moment where she could stop catching the image, her fingertip continued its downward motion, and the photo was on her memory card.

Penny frowned as she lowered the camera and uttered a silent word or two against whoever it was that had no manners or any common sense; there was plenty of space around them, after all; so why invade hers.

But then she looked past the lens to see who had encroached on her and groaned.

Of course, it was him! It was always him! she grumbled as

her fingers worked on the camera buttons to erase the evidence of his proximity from the card.

Shame it wasn't so easy in the real world.

"You like trees." It wasn't a question, just a statement so she didn't answer. Alex watched her for a few seconds then turned to go.

"I have to give you something. Return it." Penny told him quickly.

"I nearly asked Georgia to do it, but I hate being a coward."

His right eyebrow flicked up and she nearly baulked.

"I found it. In my room in Vegas." Alex was still frowning. "Here!" she held out his ring, between her forefinger and thumb, and waited for him to take it.

"You've had it a while." He told her as his hand moved up and took back his property.

"I know, I just found it again; in my suitcase." That was a lie. She'd found it on her finger this morning and any excuse she could give him for it being there would sound suspicious; so, she didn't give him one. "It's a lovely ring." She told him as he played with it before slipping it back onto his little finger. (Left hand she noticed.)

"A present from my mum." He said as his eyes came up and latched onto hers.

"So, it has sentimental value, sorry I didn't get it back to you sooner."

"Can't say 'no problem' because there is one." Alex was glaring at her now, like she was a thief.

"I didn't steal it."

"So, you say."

Penny sighed. Long and hard then... "Stay away from me Mister Sterling." She told him "I'm done with you." then she turned her back on him and walked into the trees.

8

WEDDING DAY

The wedding ceremony had been a beautiful thing. Rob had placed the ring that Penny had designed onto Georgia's' finger, they'd kissed and then they and the congregation had made their way to the nearby hotel for the wedding reception. Penny and Alex touched shoulders several times, managed to smile while the photographer's lens snapped at them; and then they ignored each other for the rest of the day and night.

At two o'clock the following morning Penny couldn't sleep so she went downstairs to her workshop, flicked on the overhead lights and walked over to a large object that stood in the corner. She stood in front of it for several minutes then tugged off the dark green tarpaulin that covered it.

He was nearly finished.

Nearly.

Just a bit more work on his eyes and front and he'd be ready for a quick sanding and good covering of wood preservative.

Penny picked up a sharp wood chisel and small mallet and started whittling away at the wood around the eyes. Her fingers checked the area as she worked, and her eyes flicked here and there deciding where the chisel would go next.

And then the hours ticked by as she concentrated on what she was doing.

Alex was in the dining room when she walked wearily past the door at eight in the morning. He downed his coffee quickly then pushed back his chair and set off to speak to her, but when he stepped into the hallway she was already out of sight.

Which was just as well, he decided. There was no use in pursuing something that was so obviously wrong. She lived at home, leeched off her mother and took things that weren't hers; she was a beautiful dark-haired cat that, in truth, was really a cat burglar.

He didn't have to think twice to know he wanted nothing to do with someone like that.'

Ten minutes later he left.

Penny was asleep when he got into his car and drove way.

They didn't see each other again for a fortnight.

Hen and Stag Do. *Bachelor/bachelorette party* number two.

Millie had called, two weeks after Georgia's wedding, and told Penny that she and Bertie were getting married.

In six weeks.

In two weeks, they were going to have their dos in Paris.

She loved Penny like a sister, so she had to be there.

Penny couldn't say no, and so, two weeks later, she'd be joining the rest of the guys and girls by the Eiffel Tower.

The same guys and girls that had travelled to Vegas.

But she wasn't going to drink, not this time.

Not because she didn't want to but because she couldn't.

Bertie called Alex and told him the same thing. He valued him as a friend, he said, and would like to have him at his prenuptial, nuptials in Paris. The city of love or was that Venice? *Shrug,* please come.

Alex, who didn't give himself time to think about his answer, but later wished he had, said yes, he'd be there, with bells on, but no ring.

Two weeks later Penny and Georgia had business in Paris so were already in the city when the rest of the party arrived. They'd cancelled their booking with their usual hotel and extended the one that Millie had made for them in the other. They'd been there for two days, overseeing the launch of Penny Craig's new line and would remain for a couple of days after the partying was over. Rob went straight to Georgia's room, dropped off his case, sent a txt to his wife telling her that he had arrived then freshened up before heading down-stairs to the small bar at the back of the hotel.

Laura and Ashley checked into their room, freshened up under the shower then joined Rob and Alex at the bar.

Later, when everyone had checked in and cleaned up, they ate from the hotel menu in the cosy restaurant that smelled like French Lavender and home cooking.

The men had steaks and a bottle of wine, the women ate chicken or fish and stuck to still or fizzy water. Alex thought that that would change when they were out on the town the next night, so wasn't unduly puzzled by the female choice of anything menu related verses those of the men.

But the next night...

"What's going on Rob?" Asked Alex around the rim of a wine glass.

"On?"

"With them? "He nodded towards the women "no alcohol."

"Georgie and Millie are pregnant." He grinned, "Laura obviously isn't, though she'd never pass up a wine glass or two if she were."

"And C.J.?" Alex let his eyes rest on that female but returned them to Rob when he answered.

"She doesn't usually drink."

"She doesn't?"

"She has a busy week coming up so won't be drinking anything alcoholic only water or juice, she needs to keep a clear head, not that she usually fuzzes it up with alcohol when she isn't doing business." Rob frowned at Alex then said, "So don't offer it to her or pour it out for her."

"Or hold a bottle to her lips till she swallows it." Alex murmured.

"Yeah, or that."

"We're meeting with Francois tomorrow." Penny smiled as she laid her knife and fork onto her empty plate. "He's going to send his car to pick us up and bring us back. He lives outside of Paris, near a lovely village and says he's happy for you all to come too but if you want to go somewhere else, I can meet you there later. "

"Francois?" Alex was looking at C.J. She was ignoring him.

"A friend." Georgia answered.

"Well, I'm in." Rob glanced at Georgia, and she smiled at him. Bertie and Millie and Laura and Ashley agreed it would be nice and Alex just gave a nod of his head.

"Okay." Penny gave a half smile then pushed her chair back "I'm going for a walk before I turn in. Company welcome." She added, then she left the room.

The next morning, they ate breakfast early then sat at the

small tables on the terrace in the warm sun. At nine o'clock they went to the front of the hotel, got into a long black limousine and settled back for the two-hour trip.

"So C.J." Laura set her eyes on the female in question and gave a half smile.   "This man of yours."

"Yes." The word almost came out on a sigh because whatever was to follow was sure to be unkind.

"Does he know about your propensity to break things?"

Penny remained silent.

"He must have a lot of nice things in his mansion which…"

"Yes, he has and they're going to be super safe today."

Penny tilted her head and gave a small smile then added,

"You aren't going inside so there won't be any accidents. Francois has arranged lunch for us outside at one thirty . He won't be joining us as he has to be somewhere else after our meeting."

"Very convenient." Laura, who was not amused before, had now moved into annoyance. (Someone or something was going to suffer.)

Georgia let her eyes remain on the woman and made a mental note to distance herself from her, and quickly, because her incessant poking at Penny was getting on her nerves and being pregnant had nothing to do with it.

The car stopped outside the door to a beautiful building that sat quietly in the warm sunshine. The driveway, that had started a mile away, continued around the side of the mansion where it terminated in the grounds behind it. Four long steps led up to the black double doors and its shining adornments, but they didn't have to knock because it had opened as soon as the car had stopped and a smart, middle-aged woman had stepped out to greet Georgia and Penny with a few friendly words and a warm embrace; after which the two women disappeared inside leaving the others to the administrations of another female and the chauffeur.

"He was very handsome." Millie was grinning at Penny as the limousine drove away from the building and Penny smiled back.

"Probably smells of onions and garlic." Laura smiled but her eyes were dark and broody. "Am I right C.J.? I mean you've kissed him, right?"

"Never had the inclination, so no."

"What's his name?" Alex tried not to sound too interested.

'Don't you start' Penny thought as she tried hard not to kick him. Succeeded and said, "Francois Falcon."

"Never heard of him."

"He'll be heartbroken."

"What does he do?"

"He's French."

"Is that a profession?"

"He's a singer." Georgia came to her aid.

"A singer! In a band?"

"No."

Alex looked blank

"Err."

Nothing.

"A crooner?"

Alex shrugged.

"Okay. How about R and B, heard of that?"

Alex nodded.

"He sings like that only in French."

Penny flashed Alex an 'I don't believe it' kind of look then flicked her eyes away from him and onto the passing trees and fields.

"I have to go into the city for a couple of hours." She told them as she continued to look out of the window.

The words bounced off the thick glass back into the silent car.

"I shouldn't be long."

"Want some company?" Millie smiled at her and she relaxed a little.

"If you want to come too Millie that's okay, it's not recreational though it's business."

"You work C.J.?"

Dark glasses covered Laura's eyes. Penny itched to swipe them from her face and poke her in the eye with them. She ignored her instead.

"Thierry will drop you all by Le Jardin. I can meet you there when I'm finished."

"I shan't be in Le Jardin when there are so many more fashionable places to be." Laura was glaring at Penny; Penny continued to look out of the window.

Millie touched her arm and gave her a smile.

"Message me when you're done, and I'll let you know where we are. We can meet you, have a coffee and then go back to the hotel for dinner."

Penny gave a quick nod of her head and allowed herself to smile.

Dinner was early at seven. The food was great, and the conversation light-hearted and friendly. Then, at nine thirty the group split in two. The men, and Laura, went out on the town to celebrate, because that's what they had gone there to do Laura moaned; while Georgia, Millie and Penny stayed at the hotel and drank water, then tea and finally cocoa before they went to bed.

Georgia and Penny had discussed the business of the afternoon then moved on to the important meetings coming up over the following few days.

Millie sat with her eyes wide and mouth open as she learned more about what C.J. did with *her* life while *she* lived her own.

"We all thought you just lived at home, lazing away your time and days."

Millie gave Penny a look that said sorry as her lips said the words.

Then... "But I liked you anyway." she added with a smile.

Penny hugged her goodnight in front of her door.

"It's okay Millie." She said as she started to turn away "Just don't tell Laura, ay, I'd hate to spoil her fun."

"I won't but then I won't be seeing much of her, after the wedding of course." Penny didn't ask why, she just smiled then went to her room.

The insistent knocking on her door finally woke Penny up. She switched on the sidelight then dropped her feet onto the thick carpet.

"Yes?" She asked quietly when she reached the door.

"Penny, Penny it's me." The voice was muted but somewhat urgent.

"What do you want Rob, its late?"

"Can you open your door?"

"Yes."

He waited a few seconds. "Then, will you?"

"Okay." She opened the door a couple of inches and peered through the gap.

Rob stood about six inches away from her and he was holding onto Alex; whose knees were dangerously bent, and his chin poked into his shirtfront.

She opened the door wider, and Rob staggered in with him.

"He's had an accident."

"So, you brought him here, to my room, are you mad?"

"I couldn't take him to ours, Georgia needs her sleep."

(She's not the only one.)

"She'd have helped you, Rob."

"I know but I don't want to put her under any stress. It's not good when you're pregnant."

(So, I've been advised, yet here you are.)

"Anyway, you know a bit about first aid, so I thought that this was the best place to bring him."

"I only treat burns Rob and I haven't had to do it in a long time."

"Please Pen! You'll know what to do you always do."

Penny took a deep breath in through her nose and out again then she succumbed.

"On the bed." She motioned to the rumpled bedding then opened the middle drawer of the chest that stood against the wall and took out a small first aid kit.

"You came prepared." Rob grinned.

"Yeah, well, Laura's here." She nudged her chin towards Alex "What happened?"

"Laura thought it would be a good idea to leapfrog the posts along the path by the river. Bertie and me, we leaped them good, but Alex had to contend with a few obstacles."

"Like what?" Penny asked as she unzipped the medical bag.

"Well, first it was a stone or two tossed at him as he ran towards the posts then Laura tossed his jacket into his face as he was about to put his hands onto one, he missed and fell and it looked like he'd cracked his head on the kerb but it wasn't as bad as it seemed, he got his hands down first so his face only glanced off the brick." Rob was frowning at her as she inspected the injuries.

"I'm sorry Penny."

"For what?"

"All these years she's been making you look like an incompetent; accident prone fool and it was her doing all along."

"It's okay Rob, don't feel bad about it, I just figured it out myself."

"It's not Okay Pen, I suddenly see her for what she is."

"A black hearted queen coercing her minions to do her bidding, brainwashing them into believing things that aren't really true?" Penny asked.

"You know her well."

"Yes, I know her well."

"Will he live?" Rob asked some minutes later.

"Yes, help me get him out of his jacket and shirt then you can go."

"You sure?"

"No, but Georgia will be worried, so go you must."

Rob got Alex out of his shirt and jacket, and she was already cleaning him up as he let himself out. The cut above Alex's eye was quite deep so she cleaned it up and ran the wet cotton over the graze on his cheek, then she took a miniature bottle of vodka from the fridge, opened it and used it to sterilise the cuts. Twenty minutes later he looked less bloody and more patched. The bruising on his cheek and the triple row of strips, keeping the cut together, made him look like a pirate.

A very sexy, dangerous Pirate...

Her eyes dropped to his bare chest, and she frowned. That needed to be covered up and quickly, because all that bare skin was making her palms itch and her lips tingle.

Penny took out the set of pyjamas she'd stowed in her suitcase and dropped them onto the bed.

She'd given up using pj's weeks ago, preferring, instead, a very large tee shirt purchased for the job. Now was the time to put them on however, so she quickly pulled the pale blue cotton tee-shirt from her body and replaced it with her pj's; unaware that Alex had come too and was looking at the silver scar that ran down the skin below her breast. His eyes remained on her until she pulled the PJ top over her head and they didn't close again until she'd eased his head and arms into her warm, but not quite big enough, tee shirt and dropped his head back onto the pillow. Then, sure that he was comfortable, and asleep, she slid into the bed and finally closed her eyes.

"How are you feeling?" Penny asked him as she inspected his face the next morning. Alex squinted at her then grimaced when he tried to frown.

"Sore? I know, been there myself." Penny didn't smile. "We leave for the tower in half an hour. Shower's in there but you'll have to go to your room to change. Keep the tee shirt; it looks better on you than me."

Alex doubted that.

"Did you get me drunk and take advantage?" his voice was little more than a croak, but it was as serious as when it was good and strong.

Penny glared at him.

"You're in my bed because you turned into a frog last night and tried to leap a stone post."

Penny saw the pucker appear between his eyes.

"Ahh, you remember. Good. Your horseplay, err, frog play, was not a good idea, you're going to scar."

(Right through your left eyebrow. Karma can kick you in the ass sometimes.)

"Leave the strips on for a few days at least; maybe let them come off naturally. A good soak in the shower does it for me."

Penny picked up her bag then looked at her watch.

"Twenty-five minutes." She told him quickly, "Make sure the door is shut on your way out."

Alex got up slowly. His head was banging, and his body hurt and when he looked in the bathroom mirror, he made a silent eek sound; then unwrapped the gratuity razor that sat on the glass shelf above the sink. He could smell Penny's shower gel as he stood under the hot water of the shower. It was faintly spicy with a hint of flowers. He liked it.

They were waiting for him in the dining room, had poured him a coffee and stacked some croissants and rolls onto a plate with butter and marmalade on the side. No one spoke as he ate; they just sipped their hot drinks as he consumed his breakfast; and when he was done, they left the hotel and were soon standing at the bottom of the Eiffel Tower.

The tower loomed above them, dark and high.

Penny really wanted to stay on terra firma but was cajoled into going up. She made a special effort to stay away from Laura; because if one of her legendary accidents happened up there it would be a long way down to the bump.

Alex seemed to be of the same mind too because, when Laura took two steps towards him, he took five away from her. The thought made Penny smile as her eyes drifted out over the city of Paris and then she just drank in the experience.

"How are you feeling old bean." Rob gave Alex a cursory glance and tried to ignore the strips above his eye.

"You took me to her room."

"You didn't seem to mind at the time."

"I was comatose!"

"And hurt and bleeding."

"So, you took me to her room." Alex repeated.

Rob gave a shrug of his shoulders and said.

"Nowhere else to go."

"Nowhere?"

"Bertie and Millie were probably at it, Ashley and Laura were not on good terms, Georgia didn't need the stress, so, yes, I took you to her room."

"Good thing I left my ring at home then."

"You're an ass Alex."

"Why?"

"Because she cleaned you up, fixed your dumb face and

probably sat up all night because you were in her bed. And if she wanted a ring like yours, she wouldn't steal it, she'd make the damn thing herself."

"And how would she do that?"

"Why would you ask?"

Rob let his eyes flick between both of Alex's.

"You don't know." He said as he gave several nods of his head "you don't know." He repeated and then he whispered 'great' under his breath.

9

ALEX MEETS HIS WIFE

When Penny got back home there was another cream-coloured envelope waiting on her desk. It was thicker this time, as though the act of divorce had suddenly become more pertinent with a larger amount of paper.

She left it there, for several hours, then bit the bullet and opened it.

The headed paper said the same as it had the last time; my client has instructed me etc. But there was still no name for her to try to put a face to, so she placed it on the desk.

The signature papers followed quickly after, because she wasn't going to sign them, not now that things had become more involved.

The third envelope was unmarked, securely stuck and had one sheet of paper inside it. She ran a finger along the top crease then dipped a thumb and finger inside to pull it out.

It was direct and to the point. She was being commanded to sign the papers. Not asked or reasoned with but commanded.

I don't know who you are or what you look like, and I don't want to know. You have managed to tie yourself to me, but the tie will be broken and quickly.

I don't know why you think I'm interested in staying married to you unless you are pregnant and have chosen me to be the father.

If that is the case, you will supply a sample of blood from the child for DNA testing.

This can be done before the birth. I am sure you will not want to endanger your child, if there is one, by having this test done while pregnant so a choice must be made. Do the test and provide evidence or refrain and get on with your life the honest way because you would be better chasing the true father than chasing a blank cheque.

You and your mother must believe you will have a good life at my expense, but you will not. I am not going to give either of you a penny; you should try earning a living it is quite an experience.

You will sign the papers today and send them directly to my solicitor and that will be the end of it, or I will take steps to make you do it.

End this ridiculous situation now or have the world know about your deceitful attempt to defraud me. It is your choice. Make it soon.

You can be sure that you have nothing that I want from you. Not now or in the future, excepting your signature on the enclosed paperwork.

Do yourself, and your mother, a huge favour and sign; it is in your best interests to do so.

You will receive the formal decree as soon as it is available. But there will be no financial settlement.

Alex Sterling.

Penny went pale and felt sick as she waited a few minutes before slipping the papers back into the envelope.

Her hands were shaking, and her heart was pumping in her chest as her brain tried to come to terms with what she had just learnt.

"How on earth was she married to Alex Sterling? She'd never met the man before Vegas and had only put up with him because Rob had assigned him as her guardian."

"Yeah right. Guardian." She snorted then sobered.

"He was really the obvious choice though if she'd thought about it that is."

A list of possible grooms would have seen his name appear near the top, close behind Bertie and Ashley as she'd only been in contact with four males that weekend.

Alex had been assigned as her guardian in Vegas, to keep any unwelcome advances away and he had obviously failed because she was pregnant.

He'd fed her chips and shared his beer and champagne, and she always woke up naked the morning after. Which means they must have...'

"Oh!"

One hand went to her mouth and the other went to her stomach, where their child grew inside her.

Dear God!

She had to tell him.

Had to.

Her hand went out and picked up the phone and when she put it down again, she had an appointment at his solicitor's office in London.

Penny shook the hand of the solicitor man who had sent her the letters, then she sat down in one of the padded chairs at the large table.

She was nervous inside and her palms were sweaty despite the coldness of her hands.

He was late, which wasn't a surprise, he was letting her know how insignificant she was in his day-to-day life.

"He's been held up." Explained the solicitor a second time.

"By a highway man? Or, in this case woman?" she didn't smile.

"Err. No"

Silence.

"My wife loves your work." He offered into the quiet room.

"My work?... Yes... I forgot... I do work... You might like to tell your client that strange fact."

The solicitor frowned and was about to say something when the door opened quickly, and Alex Sterling burst into the room. She didn't know what he was expecting to find going on, something totally improper she guessed.

"Mike." He gave his solicitor a nod then turned to her and frowned.

"C.J?"

She ignored his puzzled expression and the sudden softening of his eyes.

"You need to sit Alex." Said the Solicitor man.

"Have I missed her? "

"Her?"

"Penelope Craig. She didn't wait?!"

"You're late Alex. Twenty minutes late. She should have left but she didn't."

"She didn't?"

"Hi." Penny leaned forward in her chair and looked him in the eye.

"I'm Penelope Craig."

He didn't flinch, he just turned a bit pale as a frown formed between his eyes. Penny ignored it.

"I felt it necessary to come here today; for three reasons." Penny continued.

(There had been four, but she was chickening out of the fourth and most important.)

She flicked her eyes up to Alex's face then dipped her hand into her handbag and pulled out two letters.

"Reason One. This is for you."

She slipped an envelope towards the solicitor then looked at him.

"Reason two."

She said, as her eyes seared him.

"You need to tell your client to stop making spurious accusations to and about people he doesn't know. My mother does not deserve to be called a lazy money grabbing fraudster. She's an upstanding woman who has achieved many things in her life, all legally and above board. She is well thought of in the community and has more money in the bank than she could ever spend in three lifetimes." Penny smiled at solicitor man as he took the letter off the table.

"It's a copy of the letter I received from your client outlining what he would do if I did not sign the divorce papers. If he chooses to act on his threats, I will bring in my lawyers and we'll see how far he gets."

She turned to Alex.

"Reason three. This is for you." She slid the envelope in his direction and as she drew in a breath he spoke.

"C.J.?"

"My name is Penelope Craig. I'm a self-employed designer and Goldsmith. I earn a living at it. I'm not a thief or fraudster, I don't know why I married you, but it wasn't for your money. I don't leech off my mother; I live with her because, she's my mum. I love her. That's it."

"I didn't know it was you."

Alex moved and sat next to her. She didn't look at him.

"That doesn't make what you did right. Your threats were designed to get what you wanted from a woman who was an inconvenience to you. Do what I want or else. Well, you've got what you wanted; and I don't want anything from you either, except maybe your cufflinks."

"I can't give you them."

"Hmm, pity, I should like to have sold them."

"They aren't worth much." Alex told her as he shucked his shirt cuff down and looked at the links.

"Err, Alex." Mike cleared his throat "they're a limited-edition item. Not on sale anywhere."

"And?"

"And a Penelope Craig original."

"Which means they're worth at least ten thousand pounds." Penny told him, as she twitched her left eyebrow at him and stood up.

"Not bad for a lazy thieving bastard and fraudster who's trying to get a father for her pretend child."

Penny paused, took a breath, and glared at him.

"I have nothing you want, ever, you said! And you have nothing I want at all Mr Sterling."

She turned her attention to Mike, the solicitor who was sitting in the middle of the stupid mess and said, "I hope the decree absolute won't be too long in coming." then she smiled before she turned back to Alex.

"Please don't say anything about this to Rob. He doesn't know it's you and I prefer to keep it that way."

Then she left and didn't look back.

~

"Mum. I have to tell you something."

Penny had gone in search of her mother as soon as she had returned home.

"You're pregnant." Her mum repeated as she sat down.

"Yes, and I'm married."

"Married?"

"But getting a divorce."

"A divorce." Her mum frowned "Why?"

"He's asked for it."

"And you're doing it."

"I wasn't going to but now I am."

"Are you going to tell me why?"

"No, but I will tell you who he is, but please don't tell Rob."

10

BERNIE AND MILLIE GET HITCHED

Penny was starting to show. So was Georgia. And Millie was far from embarrassed when she said her, 'I do' with one hand placed delicately on her swelling abdomen.

Penny had chosen her dress carefully. No pleats, no gathers just a nice cut and length and a plain colour with nothing hinting at her condition.

Georgia and Rob stayed with her throughout the service and photographs and made sure she was sitting next to them at a rather large round table.

She didn't have to look for Alex, because he was sitting just a few chairs away during the meal and then he'd sat next to Rob when the celebrations moved to the entertainment area.

He'd brought a female with him who could only be a relation because they looked so alike it was uncanny.

Ashley offered Penny his hand as the music moved into a slow dance. She took it and waited several seconds before attempting to talk to him.

"Laura not here?" she asked into his ear.

"No, we broke up."

"Oh!"

"She's met some bloke with a big yacht and car and is now sunning herself in Monte Carlo."

"Do you miss her?"

"Nope."

"Not even a bit?"

"Not even a smidgen the size of a grain of sand."

"I'm sorry!"

"No need to be, we didn't really fit, and I couldn't get on with her after she did what she did to Alex. Who the hell does that to someone then laughs about it?"

Penny didn't answer, didn't think he really wanted her to. But she did hug him, and he seemed to appreciate it.

Alex had brought a plus one with him. Yes, it was his sister, but it felt better walking into the church with someone rather than without and anyway Frances was always good company.

He was aware of Penelope Craig sitting three chairs away, but he kept himself hidden behind Rob (like a coward) and thought he was doing a good job of keeping her at arm's length. Then he went to get some drinks and when he came back his beloved sis had moved seats and was now sitting in the chair opposite his soon to be ex-wife.

"You're Penelope Craig." He heard her say.

Penny nodded then said, "Just call me Penny."

"Hi. I'm Frances. "

"Hi Frances." She smiled back then took a sip of her fizzed up, flavoured water.

"So!" Georgia gave the new arrival a quick look then turned to Penny.

"You have this idea for something."

"Yes. A new range." Penny tapped the seat next to her and Georgia sat as she asked... "What were you thinking?"

"As Wedding Belles has really taken off, I thought I could do something for babies. I've already got some ideas on paper, just need to clean up the sketches and develop the manufacture costs and processes."

"Something other than booties and dummies would be refreshing."

Frances injected then smiled and apologised for interrupting.

"I agree." Penny smiled "Most high price gifts are given at the Christening, like they are at a wedding, and most are also your run of the mill stuff like money boxes and plates, I thought I'd go for something more dedicated to baby X or Y. It'll be a long-term thing, different for male and female but the same. If that makes sense. "

"Sounds good." Georgia turned to Frances and gave her a smile.

"Hi, I'm Georgia, Penny's assistant, I'm married to her brother Rob."

She held out her hand and Frances took it.

"Frances Sterling. Alex's sister."

"How is he? His face I mean."

"He's been a grouch lately, but his face is just fine, he has this little bald patch in the middle of his eyebrow where the hair won't grow back."

"Don't we all." Penny murmured, then gave a quick smile before sipping at her water again.

"Did you say you're Rob Carter's sister?" Frances asked quickly "Then you must be C.J."

"Must is a strong word. You must do this! You must do that! I must be C.J. even if I think I must not."

"What does C.J. mean anyway?" Alex asked as he set some drinks onto the table, while watching Rob laugh at something Bertie had said. The man had not told anyone that C.J. was his sister when they were in Vegas, but he could see it now, in the colour and shape of their eyes, which mirrored those of their mother. A woman he truly liked.

"Clumsy Jane" Frances was frowning. "I never liked that name."

"Then you should call me Penny."

"You never liked it?" Alex was frowning at his sister, who was looking at Penny.

"Not since the first day Laura gave it to her." Frances told him as she shook her head.

(Penny was beginning to wish she could have a real drink, just one, to make this easier.)

"Laura gave it to her?" Alex flicked his eyes to his ex-wife in waiting.

"Yes. On account she was always falling over things and hurting herself."

Silence.

Several seconds of it passed as Frances delved into her childhood memories.

"I finally realised what was going on when she broke your arm." Frances looked at Penny with ouverte sympathy written on her face.

"Laura broke her arm. And you didn't stop her?" Alex turned accusing eyes onto his sister who did a good job of ignoring him.

"Your sister helped me to the medical room; and told the others to shut up as she was doing it." Penny gave Frances a big thank you kind of smile...

"I remember you now."

"I'm so sorry, it must have hurt." Frances told her.

Penny's shoulders raised and lowered as she shrugged off the memory.

"No more than the first time it broke. It took longer to heal again though."

"So, what did you realise?" Georgia asked as she covered Penny's hand with her own.

"I'd sort of guessed what was happening but wasn't sure until that day."

The corners of her mouth dropped, as Frances took a calming breath.

"All the accidents looked innocent and natural, so it was easy to agree that C.J. was accident prone but sometimes I thought they looked choreographed, made to happen, that day I knew they were, and I've never spoken to Laura since."

"So which arm did she break?"

Alex had already guessed but asked the question anyway.

"The same one Penny broke falling out of that damn tree." Growled Rob.

"Leave my tree alone Rob. It's not to blame for anything."

"Just for leaving your bone sticking out of your skin. "

"Well, it won't happen again."

"Yeah, three times would be entirely calamitous." Rob grinned and his sister grinned back (weird).

"Looks like you had a narrow escape my friend." Rob slapped Ashley on the back and the alcohol in his glass evacuated onto the table.

"Yeah. If I'd married her, I'd have had to check for soap at the top of the stairs.... or trip wires halfway down." Ashley's eyes had grown round with mock fear.

"Soap! Really?" Frances gave Ashley a quick smile "Surely you mean a can of deodorant or aftershave."

"Fran!"

"What Alex! I mean, men don't tend to use soap any more they use awful stinky shower gel!"

"I doubt they use that Frances."

"Says the man who used to use it until he found designer."

'I'm enjoying this' Penny decided as the siblings took each other on in public.

'I wish I'd left her at home.' Alex thought as his sister released some of his secrets into the arena.

'I'm going to ask Ashley to dance.' Thought Frances. *'I like him.'*

(And that's another story.)

"Time to invade the dance floor people."

Georgia stood and dragged Rob to his feet.

"No, you can't dance with her Alex, she's your sister. Ashley, grab Frances, Alex! Penny."

"It's a slow dance." Alex glared at Penny as the music continued and couples swayed around them.

"So, I have to hold you."

He held his hands out and she finally took hold of them and stepped closer.

"How have you been?" As an opener to small talk, it wasn't bad but...

"Don't talk Alex. You always put your big feet in your mouth when you talk."

"I just want to say sorry." He whispered between them.

"Can't say 'no problem because there is one."

Penny gave him a quick angry look then disengaged her hands and left him on the dance floor.

He found her outside, leaning against the large trunk of a tree, running her hands over the rough bark, eyes closed, breathing laboured.

"You, okay?"

She sighed.

"Sorry I'll go."

He went quiet but didn't move. He just looked at her, saw her pain and didn't know how he could help her.

"You had a hard time with Laura." He told her gently.

She didn't answer.

"And then there I was, tripping you up and knocking you over."

"You shouldn't have swapped, "Penny said quietly, "would have been less pain for me and Ashley."

Alex shrugged... "Maybe."

"I'd say definitely for Ashley, but Laura would have found a way to hurt me if you hadn't done it already."

"We had fun though."

"Did we? You said yourself that you couldn't remember anything, and neither could I."

"Can you now?"

"Will the papers be arriving soon? I'd like to put this behind me, quickly."

"You have a new boyfriend?"

"No."

"Then why the rush?"

She'd laugh only this wasn't funny.

"If I remember correctly, and I think I do, it's you who wants it done yesterday."

"Yeah. But you didn't. Why do you now?"

"You give me a good reason why you want to end it so badly and then I'll tell you why I don't."

Somehow telling her he didn't want to be married to a stranger who was only after his money and name was not going to endear him to her, neither was telling her he hadn't presented her signed papers to the divorce court yet, so their divorce hadn't even begun.

"I can't do that." He told her.

"Then ditto." She replied.

"She's nice. But then she always was." Frances told Alex as her hand went out to open the car door.

"Who?"

"Penny Craig."

"I guess." Alex sighed.

"Ashley says her mum hasn't got over losing her dad."

"Ashley says that?"

"Yes. He's known Rob as long as you have. Did you know his dad?"

"No."

"Wrong question really. Did you know his stepdad?"

"No."

"Really? You never met his stepdad?"

"He was always out of the country or working till late. We were at boarding school, and I only went to his house in the summer. Never met his mum or dad or sister for that matter."

(Mum and dad were in America. That's what she'd said.)

"Well, his dad left his mum when he was a baby. His mum was a young designer and met his stepdad when she went to his company to design jewellery and stuff."

"She was looking for a rich husband then!"

"No, just a job, she was so good at design that he insisted she be put in the lead role for a new line he wanted. He didn't see her until she was already settled in the position and being paid a huge amount of money too."

"And he married her?"

"Yes, and they had Penny a year later."

"What happened to mister Craig?"

"He died when Penny was sixteen."

"How?"

"Airplane crash. He was crossing the states when it went down. Elena Craig was a mess for ages; it's a known fact that she should have been with him, but she had to remain in England because she'd had a serious accident; Elena hasn't designed anything since, which is a pity because she was really very good. It's rumoured that Penny has kept the Elena Craig portfolio open and active so that her mother can add to it when she's ready."

"And how do you know all this?"

"I researched it on the web. It's what you do when you want to know everything about anything."

"When did you do that?"

"A year ago, when I saw Penny's new designs in Paris. I hadn't really known she was a serious designer until I was at a loose end and saw this big poster advertising a show of her work. I went and was really impressed. There were photos on the walls of pieces she'd designed and alarmed cases showing her new collection. I loved everything. She's really talented. And did you know that a special edition Craig necklace sold recently for twenty thousand pounds?"

"AY?"

(They're worth at least ten thousand pounds. Her voice whispered in his head.)

"Yes, a little totem on a corded chain, and guess who sold it?"

"Don't know."

"Laura Taylor. Says she didn't know it was a genuine Penny Craig design until a friend told her, but that's a lie. Ashley says they were all told by Georgia that they were a special piece made just for her wedding maids and grooms. Laura sold it for the cash. Just wish I'd known about it I'd have bid on it."

"Maybe she'll make one for you if you ask."

Frances shook her head.

"Penny Craig never does that. The search engine says her one offs are just that so whoever she designs and creates for can be sure it's an original and only item."

"She designs for people. Privately? Who?"

"Yes, you know, film stars, singers, princes, footballers and their wives. All the rich and famous."

"And they're happy to pay her prices."

"Falling over their chequebooks."

Frances went quiet for a couple of minutes.

"So, what's your story?" she asked him out of the blue.

"Story?"

"Yes, you and Miss Craig. What have you been up too?"

"Nothing. I was assigned to look after her in Vegas and it seems everywhere else thereafter."

"And you didn't like it."

"Why would you say that?"

"Because you only look after yourself; and me of course; but mostly yourself."

"I find that faintly disturbing."

"Why? You end long and short-term relationships when the female in question becomes too dependent on you. Or too demanding; and I don't mean asking for things like a bracelet or a meal."

Frances put her hand on the car door handle.

"I mean when she says she loves you or when she says, 'come meet my parents, or she says she'd like to be the mother of your child."

"That's because I didn't want it, not with them. My future depends on me making the right decisions with the right person."

"Your future is not just your own when you date or marry someone Alex. It's their future too. You have to think about that before you screw up something meaningful and important."

Frances opened the door, got out then stuck her head back inside.

"You know I love you right?"

He nodded.

"Then if you want her don't let anything stop you from getting her. I intend to get my man so don't interfere, I want this, and no one is going to stop me."

She closed the door, and it took him five minutes to fire up the engine and drive away.

11

THINGS CHANGE AND BABIES ARE BORN

Ashley Moore and Frances Sterling had become quite the item over the passing months. Ashley was a good friend of Rob's, so it followed nicely that she melded in with his group of friends and was pretty much a part of their machine by their third excursion. She did not comment on the fact that her three new girlfriends were all in the same state of pregnancy despite the fact that only two were happily married and the third was just happy.

Vegas seemed a long time ago; and was in the calendar sense because almost nine months had passed; flowers had bloomed, summer fruits had hung from their bushes; and the trees in Penny's backyard had leafed and borne their autumnal fruit without being noticed, except perhaps by the squirrels and birds.

Penny and Georgia had continued to travel to fulfil their client appointments and would continue to do so until it wasn't safe to fly; and when it wasn't they would keep up with the demand for Penny's work by doing more of their business connected to a computer video link or inviting the client to a personal meeting at a pre-arranged venue.

Penny had finished the totem statue and had moved it out into the garden; where it now stood in a pool of coarse sand, frowning at anyone who ventured near the flowerbeds.

Oh! And a new man, or rather, an old friend and fellow goldsmith, had arrived back in Elena's life. Though well known, as a five-star crafter and setter of precious gems and metal; Henry Petersen had shunned his old life for a few years as he came to terms with the loss of his wife but he was now quite happy to immerse himself back into all things beautiful.

The two friends had met at the launch of Penny's 'Babies first' line and had not been apart since. They were now officially a couple, a fact that Penny was more than happy with because Henry had managed to coax her mother back into designing again, and that could be nothing but good for her.

So good, in fact, that Penny had immediately worked with Georgia to integrate her mother's designs into the Craig brand. These designs were coming through slowly but as her mother became more confident, and Henry's support was more accepted, Penny was sure that her mother's portfolio would become a beautiful and amazing thing.

So, all was looking good on the Craig front, except for one thing. Her relationship, if there was one, with Alex. He had disappeared after the last Wedding party, and she didn't know when she would see him again.

~

Alex was in a state of disarray. His head said one thing but his stupid heart said something else. The rest of him was in a state of flux as he waited for reason to take hold but that wouldn't happen if he didn't do something to make it do so.

He'd ignored his sisters' advice and was quietly jealous that she had not done so too because now she was forever unseen unless they were both in the office.

He never asked about the people she met with, and she never offered the information.

She was happy with her life, and he was slowly drowning in his.

Maybe he should have instructed Mike to present the divorce request to the court, it would have gotten that damn letter out of his drawer and Miss Craig out of his head. But he hadn't and now he found that he couldn't. But she had obviously forgotten about him because Mike had not spoken about her in a couple of months. Which was a good thing really, because the man hated lying unless it was in a good cause and this, he said, wasn't.

Rob and Georgia now lived in the large house that was his mothers'. He had seen sense fairly early and had moved his pregnant wife closer to her place of work before the daily journey there had caused her any problems. She and Penny were now in their element. When they weren't talking about baby product they were talking about babies. And as they did the weeks passed and then it was time for all things involving labour and pain, and childbirth.

Rob was a star.

A hero.

A superhero!

He'd spent nights at the hospital with both women and brought them back home when the contractions were of the Braxton Hicks variety and not the precursor ones that heralded the beginning of a new life.

He'd ventured out into the night in search of sudden fancies and thanked God for twenty-four hours opening at the local supermarket.

Now he was charged with getting two females to the hospital and thanked the Lord his mother was as calm and collected as she had always been.

"You stay with Georgia, Rob. I'll go with Penny." His mother told him over the back of the front seat.

He nodded.

"They'll be a while yet so don't get yourself worked up."

He nodded again.

"Girls?"

They were on either side of her in the back seat of Rob's car, and she was holding onto their hands, returning the pressure when they were hit by a strong contraction.

"Remember to relax. I know it will be hard, but just relax and breathe and you'll be just fine."

They nodded but when they were gowned up and lying on the firm bed attached to a drip and a monitor the thought of relaxing flew out of the door and disappeared down the long corridor never to be seen again.

Georgia was first to deliver. It was as if her son had decided he had things to do and had to be out of there, his need for speed meant that he wasn't going to make it hard for his mother. Her labour lasted seven pain filled hours until, finally, he popped out onto the delivery mat at eight thirty pm.

At eight thirty Penny was still in pain. Her daughter was civilised about the contractions until ten pm. Then she seemed to go for it. Birth that is. And on the last contraction, at eleven fifty-one pm, she was out, in the world, with her mother and grandmother looking at her with tears in their eyes.

Because they loved her for her strength and her beauty and her no-nonsense reaction to the bright lights.

(And, of course, for the fact that she was their very own little miracle.)

Penny ignored the detritus that covered her baby and held her close to her body. She was as quiet as a mouse and already content enough to snuggle up against her. Penny was transfixed, and in love, and quite unaware of the aftercare being given to her tired body before it could be moved into the maternity ward.

Elena Craig, on the other hand, was as proud as Punch; she'd just become a grandmother, twice over, to a boy and a girl! (What luck)

And she'd started designing again.

Just something small for her grandchildren; (from little acorns mighty oaks do grow.) "What a lovely end to the year." She thought "Christmas was going to be the best it had ever been, for some time."

12

FATHER AND CHILD UNITE

February.

One year after the fateful visit to Vegas and they were all standing in the small church in the town.

(Well, all of them excepting two. Alex and Laura.)

It was a triple Baptism service. Robert John Carter, son of Rob and Georgia Carter, Rose Alexandra Sterling, daughter of Penelope (still Sterling) and Alex Sterling and Grace Phoebe Hicks, daughter of Millie and Bertie, who was born one day after her soon to be long term best friends.

The parents doubled up as Godparents with the addition of Frances Sterling, who was asked to stand as Godmother, unknowingly, to her own niece.

It was a small celebration; just close family and friends and a quick mention of those who could not make it when the short speech was made.

On the Monday morning after the baptisms Frances stepped into her office and was faced with a stern looking Alex. He was clearly upset about something and looked in need of advice.

"How was your weekend?" she asked, more from the need to break the silence than for conversation.

"Hmm, not good I guess." She answered when he didn't respond.

"If I tell you Ash and I are getting married, will it cheer you up."

Alex glared at her.

"Obviously not." she said as she sat herself down on her office chair and waited.

He'd either speak up or walk out.

The second option was always his first choice.

"Do you really think it's a good idea to go after her?" he finally asked.

"Yes." Came her answer.

"Okay." He sighed.

"You're going to do it then?" Frances asked as calmly as she could.

"Yes."

"Then I think you need to know something. She..."

"I don't need or want to know anything; we already have an agreement I just have to get her to change her mind about it."

"Did something happen between you two? When you were in Vegas?"

Alex just looked at her but declined from speaking about it. Then, after some deliberating on his part, he changed his mind.

"I was her guardian angel." He began.

"Dear Lord, who made you that?"

"Ashley."

He grinned at her and ignored the voice telling him to enlighten her as to why. "Rob volunteered us for the role. He decided that the male party should be made into a party with the girls so that they wouldn't be compromised."

"Well, that worked out well, they all appear to have ended

123

up pregnant, or married and pregnant; and all to someone from the wedding party... Are you married Alex?"

She didn't know what had prompted her to ask that question, but she was quietly pleased that she had.

"I have an agreement with someone that I want to sort out."

"An agreement but not a wife?"

Alex got up and left.

~

"Ash?" Frances crooned.

"Yes love?"

"What happened in Vegas?"

"Vegas?"

"Last year when you went on that party trip. What happened?"

"We got drunk."

"You were a Guardian Angel." He groaned. "Who to?"

"C.J."

She cocked an eyebrow at him.

"Well, first I was given C.J., and Alex had Laura Taylor. Then he gave C.J. a cut eye and nearly broke her toe or something, which really upset her, so I made him change with me."

"You made him change?"

"Yes. C.J. was in a real mood and I didn't want her."

"But you did want Laura?"

"I thought I did."

She looked at him for several seconds then gave a nod of her head.

"Okay, so you slept with Laura, I'm glad you told me, I can't forgive you for it; or understand why, but I'm glad you told me."

"Fran?"

She looked at him.

"If I ask you if you want to make a baby, what would you say?"

"I'd say yes."

She smiled at him, and then pushed his approaching chest back to where it had come from.

"Tell me about Vegas first."

"So, in short,"

Frances sat cross-legged on the bed, five minutes later, and squinted as she frowned.

"He does a Laura on her. Only not intentionally but it gets Penny really mad, and she hates him."

Ashley's attention had shifted, from Vegas to bed. He ran a finger up her arm, and she put her hand on it.

"He knocks her about and sends her off in a huff but then he follows her"

"Because Rob told him too." Ashley's lips touched the skin on her arm.

"And you don't see them again till morning."

"They were drunk, so no;" he ran a hand along her naked thigh.

She tapped it and he realigned his thoughts.

"But then, his ring drops out of her shirt, and he calls her a thieving bastard" Frances was thinking so she was speaking slowly. "But that night he goes after her when she walks out again... Because?"

"Because Rob told him too."

"And you don't see them again..."

"...Till morning."

Ashley chorused as he eased Frances back onto the bed and slipped his hand up towards her breast.

"What were they like, to each other, in the daytime?"

"Couldn't bear to be near each other. C.J. thought he'd get his big feet in the way, and he just kept his distance."

Frances gave it some thought but found that she couldn't pair her brother and Penny up because, judging by the way they were in each other's company, they were anything but friends, or lovers for that matter so best forget about anything like that going on between them and concentrate on... Ashley... Her eyes refocused then, and moved to find her lover, who was hovering above her waiting for some sort of sign.

She smiled at him, touched his face with the palm of her hand, and then

"Call her Penny Ash" She whispered. *"There is no CJ anymore."*

"Okay" He whispered back.

"Okay" she smiled at him *"I'm ready."*

"Okay" he grinned, then he got down to making a baby.

Well practicing anyway.

$\approx$

"We've been thinking." Frances told Alex as she walked into his office.

"We?"

"Ashley and me."

"About what?"

"Your predicament."

"What predicament?"

She ignored the stupidity of the question as she paced his carpeted floor.

"We don't know the particulars and I understand your wanting to keep it to yourself, but we'd like to help."

"Help. How?"

"We don't know, how would you like us to help?"

To start with he'd like her to stop looking so happy. He wasn't used to it; Frances was a frowner, it was disturbing to see her smiling all the time.

"Its March, nearly Easter." She told him.

"Are there bunnies on your lawn? You want me to shoot them?" he joked.

"No Alex, I can assure you that if that were the case Ashley is quite capable of doing it."

"Yeah, they'd have to be chocolate ones though because…"

"You don't want our help. Okay. Good luck with it then. " Frances turned to leave.

"No. No. I do. Sorry I'm not sleeping and… "

"Not sleeping" Frances interrupted his apology "and I feel it's not because you are doing better things."

"There's no one of interest at the moment."

"Except Miss Craig!"

(Mrs Sterling! He corrected her with a look she couldn't read.)

"As I said, it's nearly Easter. Elena is organising an Egg hunt."

"For adults?"

"It's for the babies too."

"Who are barely old enough to walk never mind search for chocolate."

"It's the perfect opportunity to be in her company. Ashley and I are going; let us know if you want to come too."

Easter Sunday was sunny and bright.

Then a shadow worked its way along the motorway and landed at her door.

Penny was going to throttle Ashley and his mate, who had brought him along without warning her.

"Mum!'

"It's okay Penny, I knew he was coming."

"And you didn't tell me."

"He's Rob's friend."

"What about Rose?"

"What about her?"

"He doesn't know about her mum!"

"Then here's your chance to tell him."

"I can't do that."

"Then don't."

This was fun. He'd looked around the totem (which looked suspiciously like the one in Vegas) and had been on his hands and knees searching under bushes as a four-month-old baby looked at him over the safety of its mothers' shoulder. Millie and Bernie's daughter was a lovely little thing, a bit drooley yes, but lovely. He'd had a hold of her, for a few minutes, and then relinquished her back into her mother's hands when she got noisy. Alex smiled to himself then stopped when Rob stepped in front of him and...

"Can you hold Little Robert?" he asked as he held the baby out to him.

Baby Robert was kicking his little legs in the air and his eyes were wide as he waited for the firm touch of a hand under his rump.

Alex took him.

"Thanks. Won't be a minute." Rob told him as he took a hanky from his pocket and dabbed his shoulder with it.

"Possets. Just been fed and fast so not a surprise." He explained as the hanky went back into his pocket.

"What's a posset?"

"That is." Rob pointed and when Alex looked down, he saw a white, curdled looking deposit on his shirtfront.

"Oh! Here!" Alex handed Little Robert back to his father, took a hanky from his pocket and set about removing the curdled deposit from his shirt.

"Best keep a lot of those handy, never enough ever." Rob grinned.

"Okay." Alex didn't know why he smiled but he did. "Any eggs left to find?"

"I think we've got them all. No need to count who's got the most though, Penny always won at that, seems to have a nose for chocolate."

"Where is she?"

"Over there with mum and Henry."

"Is she okay?"

"If you mean with you here, no."

"She looks tired."

"Probably is. No rest you know."

Alex watched as Penny held out her hands and took a small child from her mother. She kissed the little head then smiled as she tucked it against her chest. The little girl was dressed in a pale pink dress and a coat that seemed to drown her with its thickness and warmth. She obviously didn't belong to Millie and Bernie, because their girl was dressed in frilly pantaloons and a thick jumper. Little Robert was dressed in Jeans and a body warmer and was, of course, a boy.

Alex was more than a little perplexed, and why wouldn't he be, after all, there were a lot of babies in his vicinity one of which created a few questions that he needed answered.

He was frowning as he started to walk towards Penny but became distracted by Frances laughing at Ashley and then, when he looked for her, Penny was gone.

"Have you been hiding?"

Elena gave Penny an arched looked as she entered the kitchen.

"You can't do that forever you know!"

"Yeah, mum I know. But I wasn't really hiding."

"Well good, now step out into the sunshine and get them all in for lunch. The babies will be hungry, and the men starved. "

She went.

"Hi." Alex grimaced at the lame greeting.

Elena turned and dropped a hot dish onto the countertop as Alex took a couple of steps into her kitchen.

"Hello." She didn't smile.

"Can I talk to you?"

"Not sure we have anything to talk about."

"Penny's daughter."

"Not my business to talk about Penny and Rose with you or anyone."

"Does the father visit often?"

"Nope."

"Does he send her any...?"

"Nope."

"Is Cee, err, Penny involved."

"Nope."

"How old is Rose?"

"Same as Robert, four months."

"Will you tell me who the father is?"

"Why? You going to force him to acknowledge his child?"

"No."

"Then why do you want to know?"

"I can't say."

"Hmm. Well. Come back when you can, we'll still be here."

Elena picked up a bowl of potatoes and another filled with peas.

"Bring that will you" she nodded to a plate of Yorkshire Puddings as she passed him; and a smile touched her lips as she stepped through the kitchen door.

"Can I hold her for you Penny?" Frances was sitting at the table, a knife and fork in hand as she watched Penny hum while she swayed gently from side to side.

"No, I'm fine, you carry on."

Penny continued to sway and to hum and then she added tapping Rose on the back. But Rose wouldn't settle, so she excused herself and left the room.

"Your dinner is getting colder."

Elena entered Penny's room and sat on the bed next to her.

"Rose okay now?"

"Yes." Penny sighed. "She was just hungry."

"And now she's asleep. Come on, you need to eat."

"I'm not hungry."

"And you aren't a coward either. So, on your feet and let's go."

〰

It was eight o' clock and the babies were finally asleep, so they (the adults) talked and listened to a randomised selection of music on the stereo.

"Oh Lord not that song." Georgia moaned but her grin betrayed her mood.

"This has to be Penny's playlist."

"It's mums actually." Penny grinned.

"Let's have a karaoke sing-along."

Penny glared at Bernie, who was still owed a cut lip; maybe she'd give him it now, in payment for the stupid suggestion.

"The kids will wake up." She offered instead.

"We'll keep an eye on them."

Elena smiled at Henry who gave a quick nod of his head.

"If you keep the volume down, they'll be fine."

So... Kids settled... The show began...

The girls were enjoying the several pop songs that had popped up on the playlist. '

This one, was quite relevant where she and Alex were concerned, Penny thought, as her eyes flicked to him and stayed on him as she sang the chorus.

'You fed me chips and beer and I was sick.' She thought.

'I drank your Champagne, and I was sick.'

'You made me pregnant, and I was sick then too.'

She finished the chorus and was happy to sit down and turn invisible.

As soon as the girls cleared the floor their men stood and sang a couple of songs and then a smoochie song drifted into the room and three couples got up to dance to it.

Penny went to check on her mum and Henry.

Alex sat in the chair, dropped his head to the soft cushion and sighed.

He didn't think it was going to work between them. Not now. Not ever.

Maybe he should just go home and forget about her.

"Alex? Alex?"

Alex raised his head to find Frances looking at him.

"Can you hold her for a while. We're going to clean up the kitchen, you boys have charge of the babies"

She smiled and left him holding... well a baby. Penny's baby in fact: all twenty-two inches of innocence that was wide awake and looking at him; her blue eyes constant on his, her soft skin smelling of baby product and Penny.

But the kitchen was in no way dirty. They'd cleaned up hours ago and had just used it as an excuse to get the men bonding with their offspring. Henry was supposed to have Rose, but Elena had usurped him of the responsibility and dropped it into Alex's lap.

And he'd cope very well she thought.

Penny was fidgety and nervous; her mum could tell just by the way she was sip, sip, sipping at her wine.

"I'll go see to Rose." She said as she dropped her glass onto the counter.

"You will not!"

"But Mrs Craig, Alex isn't a dad he won't know what to do if she cries."

Frances said, trying to be some help to Penny.

"He will be a dad one day Frances so best he has the practice."

Frances and Penny groaned in unison.

"He's never held a baby in his life!' Frances mumbled.

(Except for earlier, in the garden, for two seconds.)

"Well, he has now."

"Mum." Penny's eyes were tired and concerned.

"You said fifteen minutes so let's wait at least ten, ay?"

The girls' flicked their eyes to the kitchen clock as they nodded their agreement and then returned them there every couple of minutes. Ten minutes five seconds and whatever fraction later, they headed back to the lounge, followed by the other women, and were quietly surprised by what they saw.

Bernie and Rob had fashioned a paper spinning toy and were busy making it spin on its thin length of thread, allowing it to get closer to the baby's fingers as it slowed. Their babies were very interested as long as they could grab the toy before it fully stopped spinning. When they did the dad's reassembled the paper shape quickly and set it spinning again.

Alex was standing quietly at the window, looking out into the garden, Rose snug in his arms, her tiny fingers gripping his index finger. He was talking to her, and she was very interested in what he was saying.

"I can take her now, we're done."

Penny was talking to his reflection in the pane of glass. Her eyes holding his firm and strong, her hands out in front of her waiting for her child.

"It's her bedtime soon I have to get her ready."

"I'll bring her, you lead the way."

They were in her room. Which, he noticed, was laid out different. The bed was further left, off centre to the room and in the new space there was now a cot and a baby unit stocked with nappies and spit cloths, baby clothes and blankets.

Penny went through to her bathroom and ran the bath, the water stopped quickly, and she came back for Rose.

"That's quite a contraption." Alex was looking down into the bath at what looked like a plastic open topped box.

"It's a box in a bath." She told him, and then laughed at the obvious statement.

Alex said nothing.

"It's long enough to bathe her lying down now but later it will make her feel safe when she's sitting up, it makes the bath smaller so it's not so scary."

"Who thought of that?"

"No idea, saw it online."

"Online?"

"Don't you search online?"

"My computer and phone are used for business, not for trolling through crap."

"And I bet your car is used to run around everywhere looking for God knows what!"

"Well, I think looking online for stuff about someone is just nosey."

"So you've never, ever searched for anyone or anything online?"

"Have you ever searched for something about someone?" he asked her.

"Only when I need to know something specific about a client. But I generally talk with them by video link if we can't meet face to face." She told him.

"There you go." He mumbled.

"I did read about you though." She added with a smile.

He frowned. "Really?"

"Yes. Before we went to Vegas, I looked up about all of Rob's friends. Had to."

"Why?"

"Well, it wasn't to see who was the richest so I could marry him for his money."

Penny rechecked the water and lowered a now naked Rose into it.

"There you go baby," she said on a whisper to keep the baby calm *"just a quick wash and you're out of there, okay?"* she whis-

pered again as her hands juggled and washed the little one with ease.

Alex watched her, and was impressed by her confident handling of so small a bundle and all one handed.

"Can you get that big towel? Over there, on the chair." Penny gave a nod of her head, and he went in that direction.

"Okay, here she comes." Penny smiled as she stood up and placed the baby into the generous folds of the towel.

"Thanks" she told him as she flipped the ends over then took the bundle into her hands.

Alex sat on the edge of her bed and watched her as she talked to the baby while her hands dried her. It was as if he wasn't there. He didn't like that, he decided. So, he went closer and stood at her shoulder as she dabbed the soft towel all over the baby's body and head.

"You love her?"

"Of course, why wouldn't I?"

"And the father, do you love him?"

"I'm not sure, but I think so. Yes."

"Did you marry me because of her?"

"No, I married you because I was drunk, and you dragged me through an open door into a room full of lace. I said yes because how could I tell the lovely Dusti no?"

Penny moved to the bed, sat down, and began the process of checking Rose and when she was sure she'd dabbed at all the creases and between the toes, Penny stood and collected the things she needed to make Rose comfortable for bed.

Alex watched as she dressed her baby. Her gentle hands coaxed the vest over the small head and had the nappy and baby grow on her in quick time.

"You're good at that." He said as Penny raised the babe up to her shoulder and gave its bottom several soft taps, to make it feel safe, he supposed.

. . .

"She's hungry."

Alex nodded.

"I have to feed her."

He nodded again but made no attempt to give her privacy.

"If you could leave, that would be good."

"Leave." He gave a small frown.

"Yes, I need you to leave... Rose needs you to leave."

Alex gave a quick nod of his head and left them; and when she returned downstairs a half hour later. He'd left the house too.

13

THE ENGAGEMENT OF FRANCES AND ASHLEY

Penny was meeting him entirely too often. It had only been four weeks since Easter Sunday and now, in early May, she was going to see him again. If she believed in conspiracies, she'd believe it was one, but how could it be when it was an engagement party.

Well Big foot could keep away from her and she'd do the same to him.

Oh!

And.

She wasn't going to drink.

Not at all!

She didn't need him leading her into the night and out into a morning where her brain was as bereft of memory as her body was of clothing.

"Hi."

Alex handed her a glass, fizzing with alcohol. She held it for several minutes then put it, untouched, onto a passing tray.

"You don't need to stay with me Alex, go find someone."

"I don't mind." He sipped his drink and smiled at someone he knew.

"You really don't need to stay!"

Alex thought he did. He'd caught a glimpse of Laura, hanging on to someone's arm so he wanted to stay close to her, just in case.

"Laura's here." He told her and saw her shrug.

"She'd have to be an idiot if she tried something in this crowd."

"I'd say it's a pretty good place to get away with it!" He gave her a quick look then moved away to find Frances.

"Well, well; look who's here, didn't know you were a friend of Frances."

Laura sashayed her way up to Penny and stood in front of her, blocking her view, trying to make her feel uneasy.

"Ashley's actually." Penny smiled. "Who's your friend?"

"His name is Nick. Bryant. His dad owns a big financial company. Does lots of work with Alex Sterling. He was invited and brought me along."

(No friends here then.)

"I know Mister Bryant. He's a really nice man."

"Nick says he doesn't know you." Laura gave a shrug of her shoulders. "...so."

"Not Nick his father; and mother actually."

Penny watched the frown appear between Laura's eyes and her heart flipped. She'd have to be on her guard after all because Laura was starting to look anxious and that meant she was going to do something, stupid...

Life was never easy around Laura, Penny decided, so how was she going to put some distance between them?

The problem solved itself when they suddenly surrounded her.

Bernie and Millie, Rob and Georgia and Alex, all five adults and three babies created a buffer against the antics of one woman.

How sad was it that the act of enjoyment could be quashed in five seconds!

∾

Ashley and Frances had welcomed everyone and then let them all enjoy the party as they mixed and mingled and, finally, spent time with the Vegas mob.

Bernie and Millie had been sitting shotgun for a couple of hours and Penny was feeling guilty about it.

"Give me Grace and go have a dance, will you?" she told them as she held her hands out for the baby.

"And don't come back till you've had at least three slow ones."

She smiled as they left her and dropped her attention to Grace, who was lying peacefully in her arms.

But, when Laura sat next to her and grinned at her, Penny felt herself grow tense as she tried to shield the little girl.

"A baby, how sweet." Crooned Laura.

"Go away Laura I'm not in the mood."

"Can I hold her?"

"Can a pig fly?"

"They left her with you, is that safe?" Laura asked with an annoying lack of concern.

"Safer than the crown jewels in the tower." Alex said and as he sat down next to Penny, he heard her sigh of relief.

"The guardian Angel appears." Laura smirked. "What *DID* you both get up to in Vegas?"

"We ate food and played the slots, isn't that right Penny?"

Alex was looking at Laura like she was a snake.

"Yes." Penny was looking down, giving her attention to Grace, who was starting to fuss.

"We played the machine at the end of the street and won the big prize."

Penny's brow furrowed as her brain went into *WHAT* mode.

WHAT street.

WHAT machine.

WHAT money.

And then there was *WHY!*

WHY had she said that?

WHY hadn't Alex told her about it before?

WHY did she remember now?

WHY hadn't Alex handed over her share of the winnings?

Then... denial.

They hadn't won anything, because they didn't play the big machines, not alone and not together. They couldn't stand each other. Sheee couldn't stand him. So why would she go anywhere with him.

Why would she go anywhere with him? Her thoughts repeated.

Why would she...

"A hundred thousand dollars." Alex said as he smiled at her.

Which made Penny blink because she knew, she knew he was aching to ask her some questions... Penny cleared her throat and...

"We won some money," she admitted "we drank Champagne as we walked back to the hotel and then I went to bed."

Penny looked at Alex who was steadily looking back at her.

"Was a good night I think." She said as her gaze drifted off him.

"Yeah." He agreed "It was a good night."

Laura was looking at them with suspicion and would have continued with her unwanted intrusion, but her date put his hand on her waist, and she left them without complaining. Thank God!

"You owe me fifty thousand dollars." Penny didn't look at Alex.

"It's not so much in pounds." He told her.

"Then you owe me whatever it is in pounds."

She turned her head towards him and looked him in the eye.

"It's been over a year, and you didn't give me my share."

"I didn't know how to, by the time I found the cheque I'd already said I wouldn't give you a penny."

"So, you kept it."

"I invested it."

"Really."

"Yes."

"Well, you can un-invest it, give it to a charity or something I don't want it."

"I'm not going to do that."

"Why not?"

"Because it's yours fair and square."

She smiled then, a slow bemused smile...

"Guess the shoes on the other now foot ay?" Penny told him. "I mean, you accused me of being a money grabber, now I can accuse you of being (not a thief) one too."

They fell silent for a few minutes then Penny sighed.

"I'm getting pretty fed up with this. I don't want to hate you anymore."

"Hate?" Alex questioned.

Penny shrugged

"Dislike." She amended.

"Dislike?" Alex let his head nod several times then he brought his eyes to Penny's and said, quietly, almost lovingly...

"And yet, Penny Sterling, I find I don't dislike you at all."

And her heart raced then, like a set of mini drums being tapped at speed.

Bernie and Millie came back and somehow, Penny ended up on the dance floor with Alex. He placed a hand on her waist, under the place where the long scar ended, and imagined he was touching it.

"You have a scar."

"Yes, from the tree."

"It's quite long, a silver line that starts here."

He laid his hand on her ribcage and she frowned as she remembered the sensual sensation of someone touching her there before.

"You got it when you fell out of the tree, it cut you as you fell and then you broke your arm. You were rescuing your cat, Harry."

"How do you know that? Did Rob tell you?"

Alex shrugged, because he didn't know for sure himself; the memory was like the others that had been slipping back into his consciousness; and as each one returned, they led in one direction.

He and Penny had gone to bed, together, had had sex and, God help him, had made a child.

"I'm going to the ladies room." Penny told him as they walked off the dance floor.

"I'll just be a minute."

"You want Georgia to go with you?" Alex asked, concern weighing down his words.

"No. I'm big enough to go alone." Penny didn't smile; she just left him looking at his watch.

Penny was on her way out of the ladies room, eight minutes later, when Laura walked in.

She stood in the doorway, a tall, bronzed specimen of a woman who had something on her mind. Penny gave her a quick smile and tried to move past her, but the woman didn't budge.

"Finally. You're alone." Laura purred.

"You have something on your mind Laura?"

"Ashley was mine until she stole him."

"You left him Laura. Went to Monaco or somewhere."

"I was teaching him a lesson."

"Well, that went well for you."

"It's not going to last. Not now I'm back."

"It's their engagement party Laura."

Laura shrugged. "Doesn't mean anything. I'm back and he's mine."

"Ashley is a nice guy who saw the light where you were concerned Laura..."

"You told him lies about me!" Laura hissed, and Penny could almost see the forked tongue that rested in her mouth.

"I didn't tell him anything Laura, he saw it all for himself, now move aside because I'm leaving."

The first he knew that something was wrong was when he saw Laura, walking quickly away from the entrance to the toilets. She was smiling, looking pleased with herself. He looked at Georgia and Millie who glanced at each other before getting to their feet and heading for the lady's room. Alex looked at his watch. Penny had been gone for nearly twenty minutes. Not long if a woman wanted to redo her face but Penny didn't, so where was she?

Millie and Georgia stepped into the toilet area and immediately dropped to their knees. Penny was unconscious, lying in the doorway, her arm bent under her body, blood trickling down her jaw from a cut on her eyebrow.

Georgia turned to Millie and told her to get Alex. "Quickly!" and barely a minute had passed before he was there, checking Penny's pulse to see if she was still with them.

Several more minutes later the hotel doctor checked Penny over where she lay on the tiled floor, and afterwards told them what they already knew, she'd suffered a bang to the head that had knocked her out. She wasn't in a serious condition so didn't need to go to the hospital. He expected her to wake up when her body wanted her to, which would be between ten minutes and a couple of hours. She should be put to bed to recover and kept quiet to help with the headache.

"Give pain killers, that's all." He told them and then he left.

Alex slipped his arms under Penny's knees and shoulders and stood up with ease then he carried her to her hotel room and laid her gently on the bed.

"I can undress her Alex." Georgia told him as she took the large t-shirt from the bag that had been dropped by the wall.

"It'll just take a few minutes. You want to wait outside?"

Alex shook his head.

"Okay, then wait over there."

Georgia pointed to a chair in the corner of the room then turned her attention to Penny.

Alex looked at Penny with concern and frowned at Georgia.

"Do you think we should call the police?" He said concerned.

Georgia raised her eyebrows and shook her head. "We don't have any proof of what Laura did." She tucked Penny in. "Best not call them, lets just make Penny comfortable.

Ten minutes later Penny lay dressed in a large t-shirt, unconscious but peaceful. So Georgia told Alex not to worry about Rose then left them alone.

Alex drew his eyes over Penny's face and frowned, the cut to her brow was still seeping blood while the earlier blood flow had dried in a long line on her cheek. The doctors had attended to her but she was still in need of first aid, so he picked up Penny's bag and opened it quickly. He knew what he was looking for, found it then pulled it out and opened it.

The first aid kit, that was an essential item for Penny, held everything he needed to patch her up, so he began with a sterile wipe to clean around the wound and get rid of the blood in her eyebrow and when it was thoroughly cleaned, he sealed the split with a couple of strips and stuck a small square of plaster over the top of the wound.

She had a matching pair now because both eyebrows were damaged and scarred.

Alex frowned as he looked down at her.

'It would be quite funny' he thought *'if it wasn't so serious'*.

Swallowing down his growing anger he took another wipe and got rid of the dry blood on Penny's cheek and jaw before he left her and settled into a chair to wait.

One hour and twenty-seven minutes later she started to come to, which was just as well because at ninety minutes Alex was going to call an ambulance.

He puffed out his relief then moved to the side of the bed and squatted down.

"Mum, do we have any peas?" Penny whispered as her eyes flicked open then shut.

"Peas?" Alex whispered back as he ran a hand through the tangle of her hair, pushing it back from her face.

"For the bruises... And swelling"

"You have bruises?"

Penny tried to nod but the pillow wouldn't allow it.

"On my face and my elbow."

Alex checked her elbow and frowned; there was nothing there.

"Your elbow is fine love." He whispered next to her ear.

"It's fine?"

"Yes love."

"And my face?"

"Looks good to me."

"Okay well I don't want the peas then." She told him and fell unconscious again.

Alex was getting hungry, and thirsty but the snacks and water in the fridge wouldn't do anything for him.

"Room service," he thought as he got up and walked to the phone.

"Why are you here?" Penny demanded as his shadow moved across her vision.

"I'm returning the favour." He told her as he continued towards the phone.

"I don't want a favour from you so you can go."

"Too late. I already patched your eye and wiped your face."

"Thanks." Penny didn't smile and wasn't looking at him as she asked...

"Where's Rose?"

"Georgia has her, and Frances is there too." he told her.

"Oh... Okay."

"If you aren't good with it, I can go and get her for you."

"No, I'm good with it."

"Ok... so are you hungry? I'm starving. Let's see what they can bring us."

"I don't want food Alex Sterling; I want you to go."

Alex ignored her and...

"I'll let Georgia know you're okay then we can eat and keep each other company." He told her which made Penny feel more than a little anxious about him, because he was there, in her hotel room, and only one thing ever happened when they were together like this.

"Please just go." She whispered as she closed her eyes.

But he didn't leave and was sitting on the edge of the bed when there was a knock on the door.

Alex pulled it open and stood back to allow their friends into the room.

"How is she Alex?" They chorused as they entered.

"Awake and antsy." He answered with a wry smile.

"Did she say what happened?" Millie asked.

"Nope, not talking to me."

"Has she eaten anything?" Georgia questioned next.

"Waiting for room service to deliver. Scrambled eggs and toast and sweet tea."

"That's not going to fill you up man." Bernie grinned at him.

"Yeah, I know, I'm having burger and chips."

"And a beer?"

"Cola I think."

"You can go if you want to Alex, we can stay with Penny." Georgia told him after she'd assured Penny that Rose was safe with Frances.

(And after reading Penny's lips begging her to get Alex out of there.)

"It's okay Georgia, I'll stay, you all need to get your kids to bed soon and that won't happen if you stay here." Alex answered as he looked at Penny who was trying hard to convince everyone that she didn't want the fuss she just wanted to go home, with Rose. But everyone ignored her and left when room service arrived and after they'd gone Alex placed the eggs in front of Penny and watched as she looked at them as if they were some kind of alien concoction...

"Why did you order me this when you know I like a burger and fries?" she asked.

"Something light would be better for you." Alex tried to reason with her but when he saw her frown he took her plate away.

"We can share mine if you like" he told her as he cut the burger into four then put a quarter onto the plate with the omelette and sprinkled some chips on the top.

"I really don't want egg." Penny told him as her eyes shifted between the fast food and chicken eggs.

"This is yours." He grinned as he placed the three triangles of burger with a hefty portion of chips in front of her. "If you need any help with it just ask and I'll come eat some."

"I'll be fine." She murmured. "Just fine."

He didn't think she would be, so he wasn't surprised when she swallowed down some fries then stopped eating.

Was she thirsty?

Had she swallowed some chips and they'd stuck in her dry throat?

Was she going to choke to death?

"Are you okay Penny?"

"Could I have some cola please I can't get the chips down."

She gave a couple of dry swallows and held out a hand to hurry him along.

"You want some help with them?" he asked as he took hold of the cola glass.

"I just want the cola." She mumbled as the potato made itself felt against her windpipe.

Alex held the cup out to her as she raised a hand to get rid of the chips that were sticking out of her mouth, but he stopped her, then dipped his head, covered the chips with his mouth and bit through them, leaving his lips on hers for a few seconds before moving away.

Penny's eyes turned to slits as she looked at him.

"You've done that before." She told him as the chips hung around in her throat.

"Several times I think." She added a moment before the cola hit the obstruction and moved it, making her eyes water.

"Yes." Alex gave a nod of his head. "I have."

"And I told you not to do it." She told him as she raised the cup to her mouth and swallowed down a couple more mouthfuls of fluid.

"Only once but after that you pretty much went along with it."

He chewed the potato and swallowed then looked at Penny and asked her what had happened with Laura?".

Penny shrugged.

"One second I was telling her to move because I was leaving and the next, I wake up in this bed."

"Did she hit you with something?"

"No? I think she pushed me into the door as I opened it, but I'm not sure."

"Well, something hit you or you hit it because you split your eyebrow and it's quite deep."

"Dear God, I'm going to look like an alien." Penny groaned as her fingertips explored her eyebrow, then she sighed and dropped her head back onto the pillow.

Alex smiled as he touched a strip with his thumb pad.

"Just let them soak off in the shower." He told her. "Don't pull them off it hurts."

"Okay." She whispered. Defeated.

"You going to eat your burger?"

Penny shook her head.

"I'm not hungry anymore, I think I'll just lie back for a bit."

Alex had room service clear the plates then made a cup of coffee and switched on the T.V. but turned it off again within half an hour which meant that it was going to be a long night sitting in the chair, in the quiet room.

He kicked off his shoes, removed his tie, and picked his jacket up from the floor before tossing the lot onto a comfy chair by the door. An hour later he went to the bathroom then dimmed the lights and made himself comfortable in the chair.

He was asleep by half past midnight .

Penny was feeling uncomfortable; she'd woken up with a strong desire to pee but had to get her senses together before she could attempt at finding any relief.

She quickly flicked back the covers when she thought

herself capable of finding the bathroom, then swung her feet over the edge of the bed and sat up, wrong thing to do without help because the blood in her head disappeared and she started to black out before her feet touched the thick pile of the carpet.

She'd only been unconscious for a few seconds but when she came to, she was lying on the floor unable to get up again without help.

"Alex... Alex are you there?"

Alex grunted, and she bit her lip; this was going to be embarrassing.

"Alex." She said louder and stronger.

Alex woke up on the alert when he heard his name.

"Where are you?" he asked as he flipped on the table lamp next to the chair.

"On the floor."

"Why?"

"Because I passed out."

"What are you doing up?"

"I need the bathroom." Penny cleared her throat "Can you take me please."

"To the bathroom?"

"Yeah"

"Okay," Alex was kneeling next to her in a second, his arms scooping her up and bringing her against his chest before taking her into the bathroom and placing her on the edge of the bath, close to the toilet.

"You going to make it from there?" he asked her like he helped her to pee every day.

Penny nodded.

"Okay, shout when you're done."

When she was 'done' as he called it, she managed to get through the door before the darkness started to fall. Alex was waiting a couple of steps away and caught her, returned her to the bed, and pulled the covers up to her chin.

Then he kissed her gently on the mouth, and secretly hoped that she knew he'd done it. Meanwhile, Penny was dreaming she was naked and in the arms of her lover who brought his mouth down onto hers at the same moment Alex had kissed her. Ergo, she knew she had been kissed... *Kind of!*

Penny felt better the next morning, she could stand and walk to the bathroom without help, not that she would get any help from him anyway because he'd already left.

Georgia, Rob and Frances took her home, told her mother what had happened then left her to fuss over her daughter and Rose.

By the end of the day Penny's headache had gone and she just felt tired.

She and Rose were both asleep by ten.

Tomorrow was another day.

14

CONFESSIONS... NOT ON YOUR LIFE!

It was Friday; two weeks after the party and Alex had come to a decision. He was going to make a go of it with Penny. He liked her, more than liked her; probably always had.

And Rose had caught his heart; but he didn't know how he was going to do it. Maybe he should speak to Elena; she 'd said he should when he knew what he wanted.

"The house is going to be a bit crazy, but you're welcome to come if it can't wait." Elena told him as she watched Penny talking to Rose while she carried her in a circle around the totem.

"It's business really." Alex continued.

"Does it involve Penny?"

"It's not directly about Penny but she crops up there somewhere."

"You going to hurt her Alex Sterling?"

"No Mrs Craig, I'm not going to hurt her."

"Well, dinner will be at seven, bring smarts we have guests."

He arrived at six thirty. Elena let him in through the door and went ahead of him down the hall.

"I have five minutes before I have to serve, that enough?"

(Not really.) "I can go and come back another day, if that works better for you Elena."

"Actually, your being here evens up the table. Come into the kitchen and we'll start there."

"Penny not about?"

"She's busy, Henry has Rose while we cook."

"We?"

"We've employed a housekeeper; she keeps the house going while we keep busy ourselves." She smiled at him, and he found himself liking her more.

"Penny's baby range has taken off like a rocket; she's had meetings all week with private clients, Henry and I have hardly stopped too; so, we decided to get ourselves a housekeeper."

"And Rose?"

Elena turned to him, a frown between her eyes.

"Rose is just fine and not your concern."

"I kind of think she is."

"Why? Do you kind of think that you're her father?"

"It had crossed my mind, yes."

"Well let it uncross your mind... Roses' father doesn't want her, he said so himself; wrote it in a letter too."

"I don't want to make trouble Mrs Craig."

"Then what do you want?"

"Penny. And Rose. And your help."

They arrived at the table ten minutes late. Penny first, followed by, of all people, John Stokes (award winning play write) and his pregnant wife Mellissa. If Penny was surprised to see Alex there, she did well not to show it.

"Hi." He kissed her on the cheek as he gave her hand a squeeze.

"Hi." She smiled back at him, but he could sense that she was uneasy.

"John, Mellissa, this is Alex Sterling." Elena smiled and indicated that they should sit.

Ten minutes later Alex felt like he'd turned invisible because all the important people were ignoring him.

"Relax Alex. You won't understand what they're saying." Georgia gave him a smile then said, "why are you here anyway?"

"I came to see Elena."

"A-bou-t."

"A job."

"You been fired, from your own company?" Rob was grinning at him, and he had to decide quickly what he should do. Smack him in the mouth or grin back.

He grinned.

"I wanted to talk to her about.... Stuff."

"Work stuff or Penny stuff?"

"Both I guess."

"If you want us to help you just say the word." Georgia whispered as she leaned forward and took a roll from the plate in front of her. "But first you have to spill the beans about Vegas."

He went white; he knew he did because he felt the colour drain from his stupid face. "I don't think I can."

"You get my sister drunk in Vegas Alex?" Rob asked casually.

"We all got her drunk in Vegas Rob." Georgia was frowning at her husband who, after a second thinking about it, had to agree.

"I looked after her like you said."

"Oooo that's so lame."

"What? "

"Saying you looked after her when you so obviously didn't."

"What! Course I did, I didn't let anything happen to her."

"Yeah, right." Rob nudged his roll, in the direction of Rose then gave Alex a deadpan look.

"The evidence" he said, "that you failed, miserably."

"We were together all the time, so I know no one touched her."

"You were both drunk when you left the club, what happened after that?"

"We ate chips and drank beer then I took her to bed... Err Put her to bed."

"Alex Sterling, did you have sexual relations with my sister."

(Did I have sex with her? Did I?... Course you bloody did you idiot.)

Alex didn't respond.

They ate dinner in virtual silence. Rob was still waiting for an answer and Alex was trying to work out how to tell him. The business end of the table was in complete ignorance about the disturbance, and it stayed that way for nearly two hours. Then the play-write left, and Rob took Alex outside.

"Penny?"

"Yes."

"What happened in Vegas?" Georgia asked smoothly.

"Your party." She smiled. (Uh oh, watch out Penny.)

"I mean when Alex followed you out of the club?"

"We ate chips and drank beer."

"And then?"

(We kissed in an alley and got married by a Dusti Beehive.)

"Then?" Penny frowned. "Then nothing..." she lied.

"After you'd eaten your chips and drunk your beer what happened?"

"I went back to my room and went to bed. Why?"

"Did you take anyone with you?"

"You mean did I pick someone up and go to bed with him? No, I did not! Now what's going on?"

"But you got married to someone and have had a baby."

"Correct. But he doesn't want Rose so end of story."

"Then why are you still married?"

"I don't know."

"Have you asked him?"

"I've phoned his solicitor a number of times, but he does that thing solicitors do, and I find I'm still married."

"Do you know who your husband is? Who Rose's father is?"

"Yes." Penny's eyes flicked to the window then returned to her sister-in-law.

"Are you in love with him?" the in-law continued.

"Hmm, I'm in like with him. He's a good man." *(Stop this. Now. Stop it right now!)*

"Is he in like with you?"

Penny shrugged.

"I really can't talk about this anymore Georgia."

"Shall I get Alex to come back in?"

"Do what you like I'm going to bed."

Alex stayed over, at Elena's insistence, and they talked about his reason for being there as soon as they'd had breakfast.

"You want me to make a ring?" Elena asked him, her voice quiet and flat.

"Yes, like this one." Alex held up the ring that never, well, hardly ever, left his finger.

"A wedding ring, male or female?" Elena asked.

"Female."

"Has she worn this one? Did you marry her with it?"

"Marry her?" Alex frowned.

"Penny. Did you marry Penny with it?"

"Yes." Alex told her calmly and without embarrassment.

"So why are you making her another ring, this is the one that means something not a manufactured one a year later."

Alex shrugged.

"How about I make a man's ring, like this one?"

Alex cocked an eyebrow at her then nodded "Okay."

"It'll be ready in about six weeks. Come to dinner when it's done and I'll give it to you then." Elena told him; then she smiled as she got up from the table.

"Don't worry about Rob" she said quickly when she remembered her son. "I'll fill him in as best I can, he'll be pleased to help out."

"Help me out! I doubt it!" Alex had spent several minutes with Rob, the night before, dodging uncomfortable questions and accepting that his future held all kinds of retaliatory actions should it be found that he had shagged his sister and left her with child.

(Rob was a funny fella really when it came to formulating language; shagged and with child were from entirely different centuries.)

"He'd sooner bloody my nose." Alex added without humour.

"It will be okay Alex; Rob has an uncanny knack of finding ways to make his sister happy. This will be a breeze for him."

"Mrs Craig."

Alex looked Elena square in the eyes.

"I'm sorry... I didn't mean to cause trouble."

"Rose is not trouble Alex; you both made a beautiful little girl. And know this, I believe that Penny wouldn't have let it happen if she didn't want it too, whether she was drunk or not."

Penny had called Alex, several times, but he was never available.

She didn't need the stress of his indifference.

Her baby line was flying, her bridal line was soaring the only thing that hadn't taken flight was her personal life. She had to get it sorted before it started destroying her waking hours as much as it was her sleeping ones.

"Mum? Mum? Are you sure this is, okay? I don't really want to go but you know I have to!"

Penny was just minutes away from leaving for the airport and their trip to New York; and was having second thoughts about it; serious second thoughts.

"Rose will be fine Penny. Go do your stuff and we'll see you at the weekend. Travel safe."

So they went to the airport, she, and Georgia, and headed to America for what would be a busy week. The first leg involved the promotional launch of her baby line, and some interviews during which she'd decided to mention her new line 'Lucky Charm'.

The second part of the trip took in a quick visit to see a client in Beverly Hills who had an idea for a creation he wanted for his soon to be wife.

It was going to be a bit hectic ... And busy... and did I mention stressful.

'Roll on Friday and the trip home.' Penny sighed.

15

THE BIG APPLE AND BEVERLY HILLS

The big T.V. was on, pictures flashing, as a voice reported on the scene.

"Penelope Craig has just released her new Baby collection in America; it's been around for a few months but is now readily available in Jewellery stores across the country. Miss Craig has spoken about a new line she is creating called 'Lucky Charm', and as expected, her candid statement has set the jewellery world buzzing.

There will be no preview of the line until the New Year, then it will appear in the shops in London and Europe during the run up to Valentine's Day.

Availability in America cannot be guaranteed but you can always find a way to get something if you really want it. "

The smile of the female on screen showed off her white teeth as she glanced down to her news sheet.

"We don't have any live cover of Miss Craig as yet, but we will be going live inside the building in a few minutes."

Three minutes later Penny was being videoed walking up the stone steps of a large building as the newscaster's voice carried on with her litany.

Georgia was at Penny's side; men in black suits with

earpieces flanked both of them; Alex frowned as they disappeared inside the building in a blaze of flashing lights.

The broadcast flicked and suddenly there was Penny, standing behind several microphones, her hands were nowhere to be seen, while her beautiful face seemed oblivious to the camera flashes and voices calling her name.

"Here we are live at the American launch of Penelope Craig's very successful Baby line, and I have to say it's very impressive. "

The female was smiling as she reported the occasion.

"I had the privilege of interviewing miss Craig earlier and must say that her new line for next year sounds very exciting too. I've been given permission to tell you that the range will cover all aspects of what we see as 'Lucky Charms' but no one will know in what fashion they will be made until they appear in the shops; rumour has it that special designs will be predominantly client based."

The reporter touched her ear.

"We are now ready to speak to Penelope Craig herself, a rare occasion indeed as she is a very private celebrity."

Alex watched as Penny smiled at the camera, gave an overview of her reason for choosing the topic of her latest range, and then moved away. She looked tired and less than enthusiastic to be in New York.

His eyes followed her retreat as his ears heard the continuous clicking of the cameras. So he made a quick decision and picked up the phone to speak to Rob; then he packed a bag and met him at the airport where they caught the overnight flight to New York.

They were a right pair, she, and Georgia. Neither one of them had slept very well as their minds were on their babies not some launch thousands of miles away from them.

They were both dressed and ready for the morning and

were trying to cheer each other up as they ate; but they were failing miserably.

"We'd better get us some Bulldog courage." Georgia murmured.

"Spirit." Corrected Penny.

"Yeah that "

Georgia's eyes stretched "and some good British grit."

"We are strong independent women Georgie; we don't need it."

"You may be, but I prefer to be a wife and mother safe at home with her lover and child."

"Oh God, don't do that?"

"What?"

"Conjure pictures in my mind of you and my brother."

"Why not?"

"Because he's my big brother, an innocent being who... just walked through the door."

"What!"

"Oh Lord... and guess who he brought with him?"

The Hills.

Georgia got up and caught hold of her husband, who slipped his arms around her and held her close. Penny gave them a moment then joined them.

"You girls, okay?" Rob asked as he saw the relief slide onto their faces.

"We are now, what are you doing here?" Georgia had caught hold of her husbands' hand and didn't want to let it go until he dropped a kiss on her lips.

"Alex thought you looked sad and might like some company." Rob said against her soft mouth.

Ahh... Alex.

"We do but we're going to be busy for most of the morning." Georgia smiled and bussed Robs' lips with hers. "You can come along if you like but I warn you it will not be riveting."

Rob agreed to go then turned to Penny.

"Got to be better than a horde of silent men in black ay Penny?" He grinned as his head moved to indicate Alex.

"Those men in black are guarding our booty." Penny said without thinking.

Alex raised an eyebrow as he looked at her and Penny turned pink.

"As in treasure." (Didn't sound any better.)

"The collection." Penny croaked "They're guarding the collection."

They were looking at her like she was mad, and she was, mad as a lobster straddling a pot of hot water.

"Just come along guys it will be nice to have you with us." Georgia admitted, then she grinned at her husband and kissed him again.

Penny made a silent ugh sound then sat down and finished her breakfast.

"So where are you guys going today?" Rob asked as he helped himself to a cup of coffee.

"We have a meeting at eleven with Gloria Mitchell. She's our agent here in New York. She sets up the previews and gets our creations into the stores."

"And after?"

"We're going to climb the stairs of the Empire State Building." Penny said in a monotone.

"Really?" Alex looked at her as if she'd gone crazy.

"No, we're taking a ride around the bay to see the sights of New York."

"By boat?"

"Uh Uh, up in the air." Georgia pointed a finger up towards the ceiling.

"Isn't that dangerous?" Rob and Alex chorused as they looked at the females who must be insane to think of such a thing.

"Not really." Penny shrugged. "But we could cancel; if you have a better idea of course."

~

They had spent two hours with Gloria who had floated an idea that Penny hadn't really liked. Opening her own brand jewellery store had never been on her agenda. It would have been a good idea a year or so ago but now, with Rose in her life, Penny didn't want to tie her time up with anything but her daughter; and besides, having all her creations under one roof was just too egotistical for her. She preferred to design a range of products for special occasions like her Wedding Belles line and do her private work. Opening a store meant pencilling in time for travel and business trips that could last days; that meant leaving Rose and she couldn't do it.

Wouldn't do it.

Didn't want to do it.

A shop in America did not fit into her future, and therefore it would not be there.

So, she'd told Gloria she'd give it some thought and then she tried to hide the idea in a dark corner of her mind, but it kept coming into the light areas of her brain in the guise of a fuzzy image of a lovely tiara sitting in the middle of a dark and finely coiffed beehive; and quite unexpectedly she knew, she knew, she could trust the beehive with pieces of her work, because that lovely queen loved beautiful works of art... just like her.

~

The girls didn't go flying around New York Bay after the meeting, not that they were going to go anyway; they just teased their men with the idea of it instead. Pretending to be out of humour as they were encouraged to put on jeans and comfy shoes before going out into Central Park where grass and rocks and trees surrounded them.

"Thanks." Penny smiled at Alex as they returned to their room. "It's been a nice day."

"Did you get some ideas?"

"Ideas?"

"From the tree. You spent a long time walking around it, touching it with your hands; smiling at it."

"Yes, kind of." Penny smiled. "The bark on it was beautiful did you see it? I haven't seen anything like it in England."

"You design and create in gold and silver, but you have a knack for carving wood."

"Something wrong with that?" Penny asked, quickly on the defensive.

"Nope." Alex shook his head.

"Good because if there was...' Penny glared at him... "you'd be sleeping in the corridor."

"It's just the size really." Alex continued. "Rings 'n' charms are so small, and totems are so big."

"The process is the same Alex. Decide what it is you want to make and how big it will be. Sketch out the design, add the pre-known data."

"Like?"

"Rule of thumb. Nose in middle of face, eyes half a thumb from the nose, mouth half a pad down, take into account the size of the face and adjust. That kind of thing."

"And then?"

"Choose your material and begin."

"You've done a lot of wood working." he grinned.

"Started at eleven. Botched a lot but kept going, and then I went to Art College and took up clay and a bit of stonework."

"Wow."

"Yeah."

"So how did you get into gold and silver?"

"My dad had a Goldsmiths company. My mum designed and created a lot of their Belle Epoque pieces, in my workroom actually, so I grew up with it."

"Do you run your dad's company." *He knew she did.*

"Well." she dipped her head and looked out at the evening sky.

"I've taken over the running of it, but the company is still my mums'."

"But *you* kept it going, since your dad died."

"Mum had an accident just before she was supposed to fly here with dad. She broke both wrists and cracked some ribs. So, dad came here alone. He didn't come home."

"I thought she stayed because you had an accident."

Penny ignored the comment...

"The accident left mum with a weakness in her wrists, she couldn't do a lot of work before it played up, so she stopped doing everything. Designing, working, smiling. Then Henry came back and now they are always in the workroom arguing about stuff and she's laughing again. I love it."

"Is there room in there for all of you?"

"There will be. We're planning to enlarge the lower floor at the back of the house. Put in a couple of two room chalets, a large and small workshop and a drive and then we're looking to bring in some apprentices soon after."

"You're going to teach?"

"On the job training. Yes. I've been thinking about it for a while. I have ideas for an apprentice website. A learning tool mostly but a point of sale too. They can design and create and use it to put their creations online to sell, when their stuff is good enough of course."

Penny flicked her eyes to his and didn't let them slip away.

"It will work well for Rose and me too. I can be a mum and a designer, it's a lesson in practicality. "

She gave him a quick smile,

"Practical lessons are good for everyone." She told him.

Yeah. He thought, *they are.*

Dinner was very pleasant. Not chips and burgers, not beer or champagne just nice wine and conversation sprinkled with food. They got on well, the four of them. No surprise really, Alex was Robs best friend and Georgia was Penny's. Everything was relaxed and nice and then it was over, and they had to call it a night and go to their rooms, but Georgia had moved into Alex and Rob's room so, of course, Alex had moved in with Penny.

Sigh.

And why not, after all, it had two double beds and an ensuite.

Rob's room (that was Alex's too) had one double bed, an en-suite and no enthusiasm on Alex's part to stay and share; so, it was no big decision to let Georgia have his half of the bed next to Rob while *he* took Georgia's bed. Next to Penny's.

Alex was being a gentleman. He'd let her use the bathroom first and kept himself away from her as they readied themselves for bed. His herculean effort would have made a eunuch happy.

(Easy for them though.)

They went to bed in silence but lay awake for some time, their hearts beating quickly in their chests and anticipation drawing their nerves tighter and tighter until, finally, just too tired to remain awake, they slept a restless kind of sleep only to wake up early.

An hour after breakfast, they headed to the airport and were on an airplane out of the city.

~

Beverly Hills...

They were there, in a stretch limo, riding toward Gee Mans' palace (His name for it.) on the outskirts of the hills.

"Gee Man? Are you kidding me?" scoffed Alex.

"Kidding as in 'he's my fave actor and I'm so bombed to meet him' or 'Gee man that's his name, are you kidding?'"

"Number two."

"His real name is Stewart Finks."

"Oh! Okay!"

"Yeah, doesn't really do it huh?"

"So, what does he do?"

The girls looked at each other then smiled.

"You go first." Georgia grinned at Penny.

"So, I took my lady to the park one night" Penny began rapping.

"And sat on the bench and I said sit tight." Continued Georgia.

The men groaned as the women tapped their feet and bopped their bodies.

"When I come back, she's in a dress and shoes." Penny grinned.

"Okay! Okay. Enough." Groaned the men.

"You've heard it then?" Georgia asked innocently.

"Dear God no."

The girls laughed and then Penny gave Alex a serious look.

"He didn't sing that or anything like it. He's very good at what he does though, supposedly, but he doesn't sing so please don't be judgmental when you meet him."

"Judgmental?"

"Gee Man? Are you kidding?" Penny mimicked his voice, not very well, but he got her drift and told himself to keep his mouth shut!

Seven Hours Later...

"Wasn't so bad huh?"

Georgia smiled at Rob, who leaned forward and took her hand.

"You were both very good. So brave and strong when...." His voice cracked and his eyes became moist.

And Alex, who was on the verge of laughing too, cleared his throat and tried to pick up where Rob had ended.

"...When those guys came out with their bare arses and hankies over their penises."

His voice broke and Rob tried to stop himself from laughing by coughing instead.

"Yeah, we were." Penny sighed and flicked her eyelashes as she ignored their failing attempts to remain serious.

"We *were,* so, so strong." She continued. "I mean, all that man bottom was just soaking up the sun and we managed not to touch it."

"A-nd you got your business done thanks to what's her name?'

Rob was at it again, trying not to break down into raucous laughter.

"Gee Gee." Georgia said with a straight face.

"Yeah. Gee Gee." Rob grinned.

"What's up!" Penny grinned back. "Don't you think that crazy names are *just* crazy fun?"

"Gee Man and his Mrs Gee Gee... kind of tongue in cheek don't you think?" asked Alex.

"Gee Gee was always Gee Gee, Gee Man, however, wasn't." Penny blew out a frustrated sigh... "But it was very good of her to interrupt her filming."

"She knew you were coming right?" Alex questioned.

"Yes." Georgia and Penny replied in unison.

"Then there shouldn't have been any filming to interrupt!"

"I was there to see Gee Man, but I wanted to ask her a few

questions, and I'm glad I did, he was more open to suggestions afterwards." Penny admitted.

"I thought your clients chose their designs and you made them, no questions asked."

How naïve you are Alex.

"There are limitations to what I can do Alex. Making gems in different colours is not one of them. I don't put gems into a bowl, whisk them together and make a new one in lime green and psycho lemon. The piece is for Gee Gee, she just had to say she didn't like lime green and psycho lemon and then he didn't either."

"We were there for four hours, did you really get everything you needed?" asked Rob.

Penny nodded.

"I get the feeling that Gee Boy is not the smartest man in Beverly Hills?" Rob kind of snorted.

"Well, he was very clear on the design and what he wanted it to look like when it was done. I have a sketch, all neatly coloured in nice gem-coloured stones." Penny was beginning to lose patience again.

"Can I see it?" Alex asked... and that did it.

"Can a fish breath out of water?" Penny snapped.

"Guess that's a no then."

"Yes, it is."

"So, what does The Gee Man do? He obviously doesn't sing."

They were back at the hotel, all washed and ready to go out.

Alex was fastening his tie and Penny was looking in the mirror, running her fingers through her hair.

"No, he doesn't. Gee Gee sings, Gee Man is a porn star. And very big at it too." Penny's head tipped to the side; her face went still then she burst out laughing.

"Sorry." Penny tried to control herself but was failing badly.

Her hand went out, twisted towards her reflection then went to her mouth and covered it as her eyes filled with tears.

"Sorry." She cleared her throat. "Oh God I can't stop laughing."

"Penny?"

Alex had moved towards her and was now standing in front of her.

"Yes."

Her eyes were still wet with tears, her mouth trying not to let a sound out.

"Just Penny." He whispered.

He was looking into her eyes as his head dipped, and then he was kissing her, just a soft touching of his lips to hers, before he stepped away.

"We on the town people?" Rob asked as the lift slowed and the door swished open.

"We have a meeting tomorrow at two." Penny said as she stepped out of the metal container.

"Is that a yes, or a no?"

"Okay." The girls chorused.

"You don't sound too enthusiastic." Alex told Penny as he took hold of her fingers and held them as they walked.

"I'm not. But if we agree to behave like adults and not randy teenagers, I can try to enjoy it. We drink a small amount of alcohol, do not eat chips or drink beer and, when we go to bed, we do so alone."

"No drink, no sex, got it."

"But if you see someone who you'd like to do all of the above with then feel free to go." *But please don't.*

Alex didn't go. He stayed at the restaurant and then he ignored the interested ladies at the club afterwards.

And he didn't leave her the next night either.

Penny was quietly pleased that he hadn't abandoned her; because she liked him, liked him a lot and it would have killed her if he'd left her to be with someone else.

When the trip home had started, they were sitting four across a six-seat row, Penny was by the window, then there was Georgia, and Rob and Alex. But the seating arrangements changed as the flight continued and soon Georgia was by the window sitting next to Rob and Penny was very comfortable sitting next to Alex; their fingers laced together as his thumb pad gently ran across the skin on the back of her hand.

It was very soothing, quietly private and openly comforting; so Penny's head dropped onto his shoulder and his cheek came down to rest on her soft hair. It was a very public assertion of comfort and security and an open show of affection.

Rob and Georgia were aware of it, if only the two people involved could be aware of it too.

16

SCHEMES

"Come into the workshop." Elena smiled and Alex followed her down the stairs to the room where Penny spent her days.

"Penny being away made it easy to do. No hiding it." Elena told him as she gently shook the ring out of the blue bag and held it out to him. Alex took the circular item and held it between his finger and thumb as he ran his eyes over the familiar looking band.

"Amazing, it's just like the original."

"Yes. It was really easy to copy. We did it in the same carat gold. It's just got to be hallmarked and then it's all yours."

"Hallmarked?"

"Stamped. Inside. Can you wait for it?"

"Yes, I can wait for it." Alex let out a long sigh then gave Elena a quick smile.

"Will it take long?"

"Not usually but I can't give you a definite date. I will call you when its back though. You can come to dinner and pick it up.

She smiled at him, and he smiled back.

A week later Penny let him in through the front door and went ahead of him down the hall.

"You're back, second time in a week." She told him as she plopped Rose onto the settee then dropped down next to her.

"She's getting bigger." Alex said in answer as he looked at their child.

"Yeah, she is." Penny frowned at him and then asked, "Don't understand why you're here. I mean why did mum ask you to come today when..."

"Just came by to collect something."

"But mum's out, won't be back till late."

"I guessed that."

"She did say she had something for you though."

Penny disappeared then handed him a package when she came back. He tucked it into his inside pocket without opening it.

"You're on your own tonight then?" he asked as his eyes moved around the room.

"Yes, just Rose and me. We're going to eat soon would you like some food? We don't mind the company. Mum and Henry have gone out to celebrate something and Rob and Georgia are spending the weekend in town."

"So, you want me to run shotgun?"

"What?"

"Stop the rabbits eating the corn?"

"What Rab..."

"Keep the squirrels out of the nut feeder?"

"Forget it." Penny stood up and scooped Rose into her arms and would have walked out only Alex was standing in her way, too close in her way.

They didn't speak, just kept looking into each other's eyes, looking deep as if searching for something.

"You have lovely eyes" she whispered as he took a half step towards her.

Lovely dark brown eyes. She thought as he dipped his head

and kissed her, really kissed her; and because her mouth was caught unawares, she really kissed him back.

Rose, who thought this was the best game yet, raised her hands and planted them, one on each of her parents' cheeks.

"I can stay for a bit." Alex let his lips caress hers as he spoke. "And I do need food. Haven't eaten since breakfast."

"We have food." She whispered back.

"Burgers and chips?"

"And beer." He really kissed her again.

"So, what's your mum celebrating?" Alex was dropping burgers onto toasted buns and topping them off with tomato and salad.

"Don't know, wouldn't say."

"Are they local?"

"About twenty miles away."

"E.T.A. back home?"

"Said not to wait up." Penny shrugged and pinched a fry off a plate.

"Just the beer and we're set." Alex told her as he inspected the loaded plates.

"No beer." Penny was shaking her head. "No one drinks it."

"You do."

"Only when I'm drunk."

"Only when you're drunk?"

"Yes. We do *have* it, just don't drink it." She pulled a bottle from the fridge and set it on the counter. "There you go."

"It's okay I won't drink either."

"But you need something to wash the chips away. Take it."

He shook his head.

"Okay, if it makes you feel better, I'll have one too."

She took another bottle from the fridge and stood it next to the other one.

"Now let's eat."

He was feeding Rose chips. Penny had asked him not to, but he kept doing it, Rose was mulching them up and spitting them out; and also dropping them on the floor. Now he was making faces at their child, and she was laughing at him.

"Alex?"

He turned his head and something soft and warm spread across her heart and it melted, because, sticking out of his mouth, all golden and crisp, were three French fries.

(I dare you, said her brain as she started to move in on him.)

Dare accepted she whispered back as she took the chips into her mouth then pressed her lips firmly onto his.

"Can you look after Rose while I clear up?" she asked as she moved away from him a moment later, chewing on the potato as she put space between them.

"Sure."

"If you dance with her, she'll fall asleep."

"Dance?"

"Not rock n roll! Something smoochie..."

"Okay, not rock n roll something smoo-chay." He left her and she took her time clearing away.

The lights were dimmed when Penny walked into the lounge, and the music system was playing so softly she couldn't make out the song. While, in the middle of the floor, Alex was swaying gently, his daughter held firmly against his chest with her soft head resting below his chin. He was humming to her, and the sound of his deep voice did something to Penny's heartbeat... and, if she was honest, it did something to other, more feminine, parts of her too.

There was nothing left to do but kiss the hell out of his lips.

Penny woke up the next morning, her head was clear, and

her stomach was as solid as any beach; but her feminine bits were humming.

Dare she look?

At her left hand.

Dare she?

Not yet, let me just... she moved her left thumb closer to her ring finger, paused a second then tested the water.

It was there; she could feel the edge of it, when her thumbnail moved over it.

It was there.

(Where was he, she wanted him.)

Alex wasn't in the room and Rose was missing from hers. Penny slipped on some clothes and headed downstairs, and there he was making a mess with some pancake batter and Rose was helping him by smearing it onto the tray of her highchair.

"We're making pancakes." He grinned at her.

"I can see that." (Her voice sounded matter of fact as she spoke to him, but her brain kept shouting at him to make love to her again; anywhere. Just anywhere.)

They ate the pancakes, that were kind of lumpy, but perfect, then, an hour later, when he was ready to leave, he kissed her, and her toes curled (Metaphorically of course.) then he got into his car and drove away. It was eleven forty-five.

At twelve o'clock her mother and Henry stepped in through the door; her mum looked very pleased with herself (and she should, she'd just passed Alex on the road) her plan had worked, now to think up another one.

"He forgot to take his ring." Penny held up her left hand and Elena sighed in relief when she saw it.

"Why would he take it from you?"

"Because he always does."

"Not this time." It wasn't a question or a query, and yet her mum was saying something.

So... "Why not?" Penny asked as she glued her eyes to her mothers and folded her arms as a silent warning.

Elena didn't answer.

"Did you set me up mum?" The frown had appeared between her eyes which was the step before red alert re: Penny's temper.

"Set you up? Not really just sort of nudged you. And I'm guessing it worked." Elena sounded far from sorry, and a little more smug than she should let on.

"We ate and he sang to Rose." Penny offered as heat warmed her face.

"And then?" pushed her mother.

"Nothing." *('Lie, lie, liar'* her brain whispered over and over again.)

"Hmm, well that nothing just waved to me as we passed him on the road."

"Oh."

"Yeah... OH!" Her mum smiled, while inside her head another plan was already forming.

"Frances, when is Alex's birthday?" Elena asked as she was ending their conversation a few days later.

"September tenth, why?"

"Just curious." Elena frowned "Is he having a party?"

"No, he doesn't do that. Says it's bad enough getting older without everyone cheering away the years."

"Oh okay. When is your birthday?"

"July first."

"Are you having a party?"

"No, should I?" (Silly question. Of course, she should.)

July First.

"Well, you don't have to come Alex. There will be enough men to pair up with the girls." Frances was smiling as her words registered in Alex's brain.

"What do you mean pair up?" He was frowning. That was a good sign.

"Pair up, in twos, for the meal." Frances clarified innocently. "One of the girls had to drop out, which would have left poor Greg on his own, but now you're not going, well, its evens again."

"And who will poor Greg be paired up with?"

"Penny, obviously!"

"Penny will be there?"

"She's a dear friend so of course she'll be there."

"You didn't tell me Penny would be there."

(Was that him talking? He sounded like Gee Man. God help him.)

"Didn't think I had to. Anyway, enjoy your evening Alex we certainly plan to."

Frances hung up then called Elena, who assured her that Alex would no more let Greg pair up with Penny than a Hippo would pair with an alligator.

Funny analogy but it did the job. Frances was no longer concerned.

Alex stood in her office, three hours later and...

"I'm going." He said as he stuck his hands into his pockets and waited for Frances to acknowledge he existed.

Frances waited a few seconds longer then looked at him, and when she did her heart cried because he looked like the child he used to be. Forlorn. Alone. Unhappy.

"Where are you going Alex?"

"Round the bloody bend!" He sighed "Out, to the party, with you, tonight."

"Oh good, that evens up the table again." She gave a mock grin "You can partner Kitty. She's a dear soul, would have cringed at being the odd number."

"Don't like cats Fran. Do like pennies."

"Cats are nice and fluffy and friendly." She told him with a smile.

"Pennies are good and strong and Sterling." He quipped back.

Frances dipped her head, pretended to think then said,

"Okay you can have the Penny and Greg can have the Kitty."

Alex didn't have either.

At seven fifteen Elena and Henry entered the restaurant and spoke quickly to Frances who was frowning and looked concerned. Then she was nodding, and he could see her say okay several times. A minute later Elena and Henry took their seats next to him and fussed with the cutlery.

"Elena?"

"Yes Alex?"

"Where's Penny?"

"She's not coming, Rose is sick, so we came instead."

"You left her alone?"

"Well only for a short time." Elena gave him a steady look. "Penny said she could cope for a bit and insisted we come."

"So, you came?"

"Yes."

"And she's on her own?"

"With Rose. Yes."

"Okay."

"Okay."

He practically threw some cash at Frances on his way out. Struggled to loosen his tie as he caught a cab home where he changed quickly into joggers and a sweatshirt before throwing some clothes into a bag and pointing his car in the direction of Penny's house. He arrived forty-five minutes later; no lights were visible at the front of the house, but he rang the doorbell anyway.

She didn't answer for several minutes and when she did, she looked pale and tired and concerned as Rose fussed in her arms.

"Hi." He whispered as he eased the front door open wide enough to slip through. "How is she?"

"Sick."

"She got a temperature?"

"Uh uh." (no)

"Is it the flu?"

"Uh uh!" (no)

"Is it a tummy thing?"

"Nope. Teeth."

"Teeth?"

"She has a rough time teething; it's become worse now the biggies are coming in."

"Biggies?"

"Never mind. What do you want Alex?"

"To help."

(Sigh.)

She hadn't seen him for nearly a month and now he turns up and says he wants to help when she's tired and not in a good mood. If he really wanted to help, she thought, he'd stay away from her for good.

But he wasn't going anywhere because he'd just untied the laces on his trainers and was easing them off his feet.

"You want a drink?"

Penny took a deep breath and was about to let him have a verbal storm when he added,

"I'll put the kettle on" as he made his way to the kitchen.

Penny put Rose into her cot, the little girl had settled down enough for Penny to think about getting a little sleep herself. She sat on the bed and waited a few minutes then lay down and blinked her eyes in an effort to stay awake.

"Do it! I can take care of Rose."

"Do what?"

"Sleep. You're obviously exhausted."

"I'm fine."

Alex shrugged.

"You've been back to the states"

"Mmm hmm I had a couple of things to do there..."

"So how is Mister Gee? You delivered his piece, right?"

Silence.

"Can you tell me what it is?"

"No."

"Gossip has it that it's a special creation for Gee Gee, to remind her of his love and all it does to her."

Alex grinned in the shadows and was slightly put out that she hadn't bitten.

She always bit.

"It is not a phallic symbol nor is it a copy of his penis. I wouldn't stoop so low."

(Ahh. There she is.)

"It isn't?"

"No and you know it's not."

"There are people calling themselves Gee Man and Gee Gee! I never knew that either."

"It's a ring. He's going to ask her to marry him in a couple of weeks. The gems are set like a flower garden, because she likes flowers and stuff; his words not mine; and he wanted her to have a piece of a garden with her all the time. He's a bit

181

insensitive to colour but I don't know how he can mistake a beautiful daffodil yellow for psycho."

She yawned.

"Anyway, I delivered it last week and he was very happy."

"I bet he was."

"I wonder if he gets frustrated" Penny murmured as her eyelids started to droop.

"He does it all the time." Murmured Alex. "So, he probably doesn't. No tension, no wondering thoughts, and no itch he can't scratch. Lucky Gee man."

The room went quiet, for thirty seconds, and then Rose shifted, mewed and hiccupped into a soft cry of pain.

Elena and Henry returned home at two a.m. The house was calm, the lights were off downstairs, and silence was everywhere.

They had a quick nightcap, of tea and a biscuit, and then the two adults made their way upstairs into the soft glow of the landing light. Henry went on into their bedroom as Elena walked swiftly to Penny's door. She pushed it open and, as she stepped through the doorway, she caught sight of Penny and Alex; they were lying facing each other, fast asleep; and sandwiched between them was little Rose; one small hand holding tight to Alex's thumb while the other held on to her mothers' shirt.

"You alright love?" Henry smiled and Elena's heart beat a little faster.

"I'm fine Henry, just fine." She told him.

And she was, because as plans go this one had gone well; even if the ending was all down to a dark-haired little flower called Rose.

17

BACHELOR(ETTE) PARTY... ROUND THREE

It was September the tenth. Alex's birthday: another year added to his age; another celebration not going to be celebrated; but it didn't stop Frances and Ashley from having their pre-wedding 'dos' on the same day.

They were not going to be held anywhere exotic (if you can call Vegas and Paris exotic) it would be held in the local town, you know, the one down the road from Penny's house.

(I know, bor-ring, no clubs, no discos, just a pub and a Fluffy Flamingo bird. *Sorry!*)

"You really don't have to do this you know?" Penny was talking to Frances on the phone; Rose attached to her hip, her tiny hands trying to grab the receiver.

"Do what?"

"Have your party in my little township. You should be letting your hair down in London, or Paris. Somewhere less not night-clubby."

"I'm not a night-clubby person Penny, never have been." Frances smiled.

Then...

"Ashley says there's a pub in your town that has stand ups every Saturday and guess who they have as a guest tonight?"

(Oh Lord. Do Not say Fluf...)

"Someone called Fluffy Flamingo. He, or should I say she, does a regular stint there every few months and is supposedly very funny.."

"Alex said he wasn't going to come but I made him promise that he would."

(The night just gets better)

"Millie and Bernie will be at your place at about seven, cabs are ordered for half past. I can't wait for this."

(Can't say I can't.)

Penny closed the phone then took Rose down to her workshop.

∾

"Hi."

Alex looked good. Rose thought so too because she started fighting to be put into his arms. Traitor.

"She wants you, is that okay?"

He took her, without a word, and stepped away leaving Penny to sigh at the inconvenience of it all.

"I'm going to finish getting ready, the others should be here soon."

Penny left but went downstairs to her workshop instead of to her room so that she could pick up a small black box from her bench.

'It may not be a good idea to give it to him.' Penny thought as she made her way back to Alex and Rose. *'But it was made for him so he should have it.'*

So, Penny fussed with Rose, over his shoulder, and eased her little fingers gently around the dark box then she moved away to talk to Millie and Bernie, who had arrived during her absence. She tried not to notice when Alex managed to catch the box before it tumbled down his wonderful body to the floor. But she did.

He put it into his pocket, without opening it 'and that', Penny thought, 'was that.'

～

"Good evening, ladies and gentlemen, once again we are pleased to bring you our very own Fluffy Flamingo."

Penny was standing at the bar when Georgia dropped a loaded glass in front of her. Penny looked at it then pushed the tall glass away from her as if it were the woman herself.

"Nope not tonight Georgia I'm not drinking anything but lime 'n' soda."

Vain effort really, because as soon as Fluffy started strutting her stuff on the low stage, Penny started drinking the contents of the alcohol filled glass.

"Are you ok Penny?" Frances grabbed her hand as she looked at her with concern.

"I think I'm becoming allergic to birds..." Penny offered.

"Allergic?" Frances said loudly.

"Mmm hmm."

"So, you want to get out of here then?"

"Yeah, but the guys are all working to some plan..."

"Doesn't mean we have to fall in with them..." Frances slugged down her drink then gave Penny a smile as she stepped away from the bar.

And a few minutes later....

"We're going to head into town. Are you coming?" Frances was smiling at Penny.

"We are in town Frances!"

"London town Penny."

"Why?"

"Because the girls want to boogie."

"And the guys?"

Frances shrugged. "Don't know, Georgia is telling them we're off, so, are you coming?"

"Yeah, of course, I'll text mum, tell her I'll be later than I said."

"Ok but don't be long, taxi's almost here."

The taxi dropped them off at a club that specialised in weird drinks, you know, the type that involves dry ice and stuff like that. Penny wasn't convinced that they were any good for her and, once the music got louder, she was sure that the place just wasn't her thing.

"We're leaving." Georgia caught her arm and eased her towards the door.

"Thank God." Penny let out a sigh of relief. "One more dose of ice fumes and I'd believe anyone who told me I was a penguin. Where are we going?"

"Don't know, the guys are outside and have plans, that's all I know."

"I could just go home. "

"You can't, Alex would be on his own and that would upset the balance."

"Oh! Well, can't do that now, can I?" (Sarcasm)

"I mean if the balance is upset the world will stop!"

"Penny." Frances was looking at her through glazed eyes. "Stop being you for a while and enjoy yourself. Got it?"

Penny nodded but didn't agree that being her was not at all enjoyable.

They ended up in a nightclub called 'That '70s Feeling.' It served run of the mill drinks and food to order. (Which was predominantly (you guessed it?) burgers and chips, chicken and chips and chips.) (And beer was there too, somewhere.)

"You want another a drink?" Alex could finally stand being next to her and she sighed before answering.

"No thanks, just waiting for Georgia and Millie then we're going to boogie our stuff."

"Boogie your stuff?"

"Millie's words. She's a little hyped from all that dry ice."

"Dry ice?"

"Yeah, I don't get it but then I'm a beer and chip kind of girl."

"You hungry?"

(Not for food.) "A little."

"I'll get us something but I may be a while."

She gave him a wry look as Frances (who? Yes, the Frances who doesn't like to night club) dragged her towards Georgia and Millie.

"Take this Penny Craig." Georgia was holding out a small shot glass with something that looked like tar filling it to the brim, but it could as easily have been pink in the dim lighting. She shook her head.

"Take it Penny. And drink it."

"First. What is it? Second will it make me sick? Third I'm a mummy and I need a clear head in the morning."

"One. It's someone's cousin. (What? Whose?) Second Probably. Third. Elena says I'm to make sure you enjoy yourself because she and Henry are taking the kids out early tomorrow, so hangovers are not an issue."

(And stop overs? What about stopovers?)

"Okay but only this one, then no more shots, I don't like being sick."

"I know love, but drink it anyway."

Penny tipped her head back and drank. The cousin didn't taste so bad until it set fire to her throat. Penny inhaled deeply to try to offset the burning and take in enough air to expel the heat when she blew it out again.

"Good, now take this!" Georgia was holding a loaded

tumbler in her direction.

"What is it?"

"Rum and cola."

"Oh." Penny frowned at the glass then flicked her eyes up to Georgia's face.

"You trying to get me drunk?"

"Am I succeeding?"

"Yes. But you're trying to get me drunk. Why?"

"Because you have lots of fun when you're drunk Penny and I believe you deserve a little bit more."

"Fun?"

"We can call it that if you like."

"Call what it?"

"You need another drink, Pen." Penny shook her head. "Yeah love, you do."

He was sitting where she'd left him, surrounded by the other three males. On the countertop was a basket of fries and a burger lying on a bed of lettuce between two sides of a toasted bun. Penny plopped down onto the barstool then stretched out a hand and took a group of pale gold chips between her fingers.

"You hungry?" Alex asked with a grin.

"Yes." Penny nibbled along the length of a couple of chips until they had disappeared into her mouth. "Must be the dancing or whoever's cousin it was."

"Cousin?"

"Or the rum. Georgia is trying to get me drunk."

"Looks like she's succeeded. Whose cousin?" Alex asked again.

Penny's shoulders went up towards her ears as she reached for his beer. "Georgia doesn't know but he tasted quite nice actually."

"You kissed him?"

"Who?"

"Someone's cousin."

"Did I?"

(Dear Lord, she was driving him insane.)

"Hi." Millie said, as she appeared next to them then asked Penny if she wanted another shot.

"Can I have what I had before?" Penny answered with a grin.

"Sure, what was it."

Penny frowned as she thought about it then grinned again when she remembered, "Georgia said it was someone's cousin or brother, or something."

"Okay"

(Alex sighed out an okay too, just before he took a large bite out of the burger.)

"Have you tried the cousin?" Penny was raising the shot glass to her lips when she thought to ask him the question; and then she tipped the small glass and flooded her mouth with the sweet and burning liquid.

"Not yet" Alex told her as he leaned towards her; and then he kissed her, hard, and as his lips pressed down on hers his tongue slipped past them and took up residence in her mouth for several seconds, tasting the sweet alcohol as her lips reacted to his.

"We need to get out of here." He whispered against her ear.

"Okay." Answered the nod of her head, and a few seconds later they were outside in the cool night air.

They entered his apartment in a state of frantic want and need. It had started at the bar, continued in the shadows as they waited for the taxi and was stoked by their intense kissing in the lift up to his apartment.

"Penny?"

"Yes?"

(Please don't tell me this is a mistake and send me away.)

"Are you drunk?"

"A little, are you?"

"A little."

Silence.

Then.

"Penny, do you know who I am."

"Yes."

"Who am I?"

"You're Alex." She kicked her shoes off then put her hands up behind her neck.

"Penny?"

"Yes Alex."

"Who is the father of Rose?"

Penny's fingers continued trying to take hold of the zipper on her dress.

"My husband is."

"And who is your husband, Penny?"

"Alex Sterling."

"And who is Alex Sterling?"

"You are Alex."

"Penny?"

"Yes Alex."

"I'm going to kiss you now and then I'm going to make love to you all night, because I want to. Is that okay with you?"

"Yes, Alex it's okay with me."

When she woke up the next morning, she thought she was living in ground hog day because she was lying in a strange bed in a strange room with no clothes on under the sheets. Her head was a bit fuzzy (slight change there as there was no headache) her stomach was a little uneasy but not in full on I'm going to vomit soon mode, and her feminine bits were buzzing. She moaned at her mere existence, then was slightly surprised when a hand caressed the scar on her side as it moved up to cup her breast.

'Oh Lord' her brain began, 'I've picked up a hobo and slept with him!'

"Morning." A husky voice whispered in her ear.

"Morning." She answered as she felt the hobo move his body closer to her, but she couldn't bring herself to turn around and look him in the eye.

"You want breakfast?" asked Hobo.

"You have anything interesting to offer?" she asked in return.

"Yes, but it will take some preparation."

How much?" she asked as she allowed herself to smile.

"Let me show you." Alex raised himself up onto his elbow and eased her onto her back. Then he smiled and dipped his head, and as he did so a small circular charm dropped off the skin on his chest and hung from his neck for a second before it came down to rest between her breasts.

Penny raised a hand and covered it, pleased that he had opened the box; overjoyed that he'd fastened the charm around his neck. Happy she had given it to him.

She'd fashioned it in the shape of a circle and had placed a small pink rose on the front. The back was made to look like a penny and carried the word at the top of it while in the centre it had Be My Good Luck Charm written as though a pen had been passed over it.

He frowned. "You, okay?"

"Yes." She put a hand up and ran it over his cheek. "Just very hungry."

If they thought they'd got away with it they were wrong because, that morning, sitting patiently back at her home, were eight people, all waiting for their return, eager to know why they'd left without a word and why they hadn't answered the phone calls and messages that had been sent to them during the night and again that morning...

18

WE ARE NOT AMUSED...

They had managed to ride the barrage of questions without revealing anything about their private circumstances and by the end of the intense hour the only people who were in any way upset were Rob and Georgia. They had gone into the interrogation believing that Alex would finally admit that he was married to Penny and that Rose was his daughter AND extoll his great love for Penny too. He did none of it; he just stood there, like the natural born fool that he was, and dodged every mine they laid, every trap they set.

What an idiot.

What a coward.

Penny deserved better than that and, Rob decided, he was going to get that better thing for her.

"She has a kid Alex. You okay dating someone with another man's child hanging about?"

Rob was being deliberately offensive, and Alex was glaring at him. Good!

"She's a nice kid." Alex answered calmly.

"Yeah, she is but you shouldn't get too involved."

"Why not?"

"Because her daddy might come and take her and Penny back."

"That won't happen."

"Are you sure. She obviously feels something for the guy, she wouldn't have let herself get pregnant if she didn't."

"It won't happen Rob."

"And you know what else won't happen Alex, you won't break her spirit and get away with it; I won't let you. Everyone won't let you. She's my sister, I love her, you need to decide how you feel about her and if it's not love then just walk away before you do them both a lot of damage."

~

Alex left the house and stayed away from Penny for what was left of the summer; then October and November passed too.

And then it was December the 22nd; his sister's wedding dinner and the wedding two days later; he couldn't disappoint Frances by not being there for her; so there he was. And so was everyone else.

Alex was at the meal; with a female Penny didn't know, and he was ignoring her, like she was nothing to him. Why he did it she couldn't guess; so, she did it too.

Talk to a man all night, that is, like *he* didn't exist.

But she felt lost and alone, like she'd been thrown into a time warp and was living the months after Vegas all over again; and there he was dating another woman and smiling like *she* didn't exist at all either.

(Déjà vu you've done it again. Bloody hell!)

Everyone stayed away from him like he had the plague; even Frances thought she'd get cooties off of him if she talked to him for too long. But talk she did.

"What are you doing Alex."

"Doing?"

"With Felicity Kline?"

"Eating a nice meal."

"What about Penny?" Frances was frowning at him, and it annoyed him.

"She's got what's his name whispering sweet things into her ear, he might get lucky if she drinks enough."

"Penny is not drinking tonight." *(And that's a bit low coming from you.)*

"Why not?"

"She never drinks as a rule it's just fools like you who ram it down her neck. And then she sleeps with an idiot and gets into trouble. So, she's not drinking and we're all quite happy to let her do what's best for her and Rose. And as for Romeo there, he's got as much chance as a snowball in hell; just like you do now."

Ninety minutes later he saw her kiss Frances and Ashley and then she left with Rob and Georgia. Romeo sat sulking at the end of the table for a couple of minutes then slid into Robs' vacant seat and tried to chat up the female in the next chair. She got up and moved closer to Frances and that was that for him.

It was almost eleven when Alex dropped his date off at her place. He declined an invite inside and went home where he picked up the phone and called Frances. She was less than enthusiastic to hear from him; after all, he'd hurt her by insinuating that her best friend was an easy lay and hurt her best friend by taking a bimbo like Felicity to his sister's wedding meal.

"If you bring her to my wedding Alex Sterling, then you can tear up my telephone number and forget where I live."

Frances was angry and had put the phone down on him before he could comment, so he got into his bed a very thoughtful man.

~

Two days later and the wedding day had arrived. A cold looking mist hung in the air and the early morning frost left a white crisp covering on the grass.

Penny got up and made a dash for the toilet. Not a good start to the day but not unusual considering her condition. Roll on her second trimester, its hello would say goodbye to the sickness of the first.

"Morning mum." Penny dropped Rose into her highchair then sat at the kitchen table. Elena flicked the switch on the kettle then turned and looked at her daughter. She didn't look well.

"You okay love? You look a bit peaky."

"I'm okay mum."

"Not coming down with the flu or a tummy bug I hope?"

"No mum, but I need to tell you..."

"Oh! Dear, what are you going to do?"

"I'm going to tell him, today, at the wedding, when the speeches are done and Frances has had a nice day, I'm going to tell him and then I'll feel better."

Silence.

"It's the right thing to do, isn't it?"

"Yes, love I think it is."

"So do I, I just don't know that I can live with the probable outcome."

"We're here for you love, whatever happens, you know that we can work on the future when we know what has happened in the present. Okay?"

Penny nodded then...

"I have an idea I'd like to talk to you about mum, it's a new collection I'd like to do... called 'The Dusti Look'. It'll be a small collection of Tiaras and other pieces that I want to reflect the 1920's to the 1940's style and settings... I saw this beautiful tiara in Vegas, and I can't get it out of my head, but I'm busy with the baby and bride collections and the new Lucky Charms so I haven't really got the time to develop the idea... I know you love the '20's style so I thought you might like to take it further... They're going to be exclusively available in one place...Vegas... and I know exactly who I'd like to be in charge of the business there... her name is Dusti Beehive... she's different, but loyal and funny and very competent... She'll choose her own staff who will all be different too, but I know you'll love her when you meet her ... If you want to do it of course... I'll show you a photo of the tiara Dusti has so you know why I trust her; just think about it ay... and let me know when you've made up your mind... Ok?"

"Ok love... I'll give it some thought."

Elena gave Penny a small smile, but Penny knew she was already hooked, because her eyes had become brighter and the frown between them was the one that forewarned the production of some amazing ideas...

The end pieces were going to be beautiful... and Penny couldn't wait.

Later that day they were part of the wedding ceremony; all of them. The maids and groomsmen, the little man and little girls. All of them; what a sight it was; and what a time for the kids; who didn't care that their lovely suit and dresses were supposed to look clean and presentable till they took them off for bed.

Bernie chased Phoebe.

Rob and Georgia chased little Robert.

And Penny managed keep up with Rose.

Then the kids held onto a parent's finger as they followed the bride down the aisle, were vocal and fidgety during the service and finally, there was the photography, outside in the cold, on the wet, muddy earth.

~

"Bloody hell I'm pooped." Rob leaned back into his high-backed chair, catching his heels in the stretchy white material that covered it from top to bottom.

"The little monster is still full of beans." Rob complained.

"He's getting hungry Rob." Georgia answered.

"But he only just had breakfast."

Georgia didn't tell Rob how many hours ago breakfast was, she just smiled as she took little Robert into her arms then plopped him onto his dad's lap.

"I'm going to the loo Rob. Look after him. If he gets away from you, we won't find him for hours." She stood up and caught her husband looking at her with a blank expression.

"Okay. Listen to me, if our son is not where I left him when I get back, I will divorce you and make sure you get full time custody."

Rob was still grinning when she left.

"Houston, we have a problem."

Millie walked into the wash area and levelled a concerned look in the mirror; Georgia frowned back.

"Alien invasion." Millie continued in her Apollo speech.

"Just saw Orpheus and his hand maiden of doom."

(Blank stare.)

"Orson Black and Laura Taylor." Enlightened Millie.

"Oh! SHIT."

"Yeah, that's what I said. Kind of."

"Where is Penny?" asked Georgia.

"Last I saw she was wandering lonely as a cloud."

"Millie!"

Millie looked at her with wide eyes and an open mouth

"Do you have to do this now? Can you speak normal

197

speak for the rest of the night because decoding your stuff might not be conducive to a good outcome." (Lord. Now she was at it.)

Millie nodded and they went out to find the others.

"We need to run interference. Where Penny is so shall we be."

Georgia raised an 'I told you about that' eyebrow at Millie and she cleared her throat.

"It's pretty illogical to expect all of us to stay with Penny all the time but I think we should make the effort."

"Agreed. That way there is always a few pairs of hands should they be needed. We have to think of Penny and her babies. Should we involve Alex?"

"I'm sure he'll help if he happens to find himself in the middle of a ruckus. But he should be in on this from the start, I'll send Bernie to tell him."

~

It began during the meal. Penny was feeding Rose off her plate, coaxing food into her mouth and crooning 'good girl' into her ear when an arc of fluid flew over her shoulder. It cleared the front of her dress but splashed down onto her lap, catching Rose's hair and soaking the little girls back. Rose reacted by drawing in a sharp breath then letting it out in a long-frightened cry which made her mother grab the baby bag at her feet and leave the room.

Georgia looked at Millie and indicated they should follow, so each woman picked up their kiddie bag, grabbed hold of their child and walked out.

Laura was already in the lady's room when they got there. She'd been hiding out in a toilet booth, waiting for Penny to show up and had already started her verbal abuse by the time the two women entered the fray.

Laura's' face was stark white, and her eyes were wild.

"He should have been mine." She was saying. "But you had to hurt yourself on the plane and then they swapped."

"Ashley asked Alex to swap because he'd seen one too many accidents;"

Penny had managed to get her wrist out of Laura's tight hold and was rubbing the injured area as she spoke.

"Maybe, if you hadn't put that suitcase behind me and made me fall over it, Ashley would have been content with his designated Devil."

"It was you, falling over his damn feet that did it, I should have stuck you in a parachute and tossed you out of the plane; and who would have thought I'd done it? No one that's who, they'd have chalked it up to silly Clumsy Jane and her accident-prone foolish head."

Laura couldn't stop her tirade even though she'd seen the other women enter the room.

But then, moments later, she'd finished and suddenly left, and they all breathed a sigh of relief.

"You okay Penny?" Millie frowned as she lay a hand on Penny's shoulder.

Penny gave a quick nod. "Just my wrist."

"Let's run it under some cold water ay?"

"Okay."

The water was cold and oddly comforting. It took away the burning sensation under the skin and slowed Penny's racing pulse.

"Nice ring." Millie put two fingers under it as she looked at Penny. And she waited.

"Don't get excited Mill. It's going back today and will never darken my finger again."

"Going back? You're giving it back? Can you do that?"

Penny shook her head. "It's the hardest thing to get rid of that I've ever known." She told them as two pairs of eyes looked at her with a question that was wrapped in silence.

"But yes, I'm going to give it back, for keeps this time. But first I'm going to clean up my daughter and get rid of these smelly clothes."

They helped, on account it hurt Penny to move her wrist, by stripping the wine-soaked clothes off Rose and giving her a warm soapy wash. The spare set of clothes allowed Rose to roll around on the floor if she wanted to, and she looked like she was pleased to be in them.

"You stay here while I give Robert to Rob. I'll be back in a minute."

Georgia smiled at Penny then turned to Millie.

"Barricade the door when I go Mill. And only open it when you hear the sound of the drums."

Millie frowned at her.

"I'll only be a minute." Georgia grinned, then she left.

Alex saw Georgia tap Rob on the shoulder then hand over their child, she exchanged a few words with him, stopped him getting up, then left the room again. Something was going on and he couldn't leave the table. Not yet.

~

"Rob says to come back to the table and not move." Georgia told the women as she re-entered the toilet area.

"God I'm starving." Millie smiled. "I've just eaten a lush meal and I'm still hungry. Last time that happened I was... Oh! Where's Bernie?"

"He's at the table Millie, where you left him."

"Okay are we going back now, I need to tell him something."

"Yeah." Penny sighed. "We're going back now."

"All must know; information must be imparted asap." Millie had lost it again.

"What?" chorused Penny and Georgia.

"Nothing. "Millie gave a half smile. "I just need to speak to Bernie."

"Then let's go back."

So, they did.

19

THE SECOND ENCOUNTER...

Alex had left the dining room and slipped into the room next-door, Penny saw him leave and hurried to catch up to him, but he'd disappeared.

Rob and Bernie were waiting for him when he entered the designated meeting place and got on with the conversation before the door was properly closed.

"That bitch has done it again." Rob was pacing up and down. "Caught her in the loos before the girls got there. Hurt her wrist and ran her mouth off."

"Shit!" Bernie and Ash breathed in unison.

"Probably soaked Rose with the wine too. Poor kid." Rob frowned.

"She hurt Rose?" Alex growled as his eyes turned stormy.

"No, she hurt Penny and soaked Rose in pink wine." Rob explained.

"Is she still about?" Alex was now looking murderous.

"Yes. The girls are keeping an eye on her but it's a bit hard when there are so many people about. And Penny doesn't help either, she has something on her mind and it's fogging her judgement."

Rob looked at Alex and frowned

"Georgia says Penny has something to return, for good this time, and seems to think whatever it is belongs to you."

"Me?"

Alex's hand was in his pocket, flicking a circular piece of metal between his fingers and thumb.

"What does she have that's mine?"

'You know man. You know.' Said a voice in his head.

"Don't know, maybe you should run her down and ask her." Suggested Rob.

"Meantime what are we going to do about Laura? She hasn't spoilt the day yet but it's only a matter of time before she does." Ashley said pointedly.

"We set a trap, maybe!" Bernie grinned with a mischievous look.

Bernie was looking more serious than anyone had seen him look for a long time. Not a good thing for Laura.

"We use Penny as bait. Laura will fall for it even if TRAP was advertised in bright lights cos basically Laura is stupid... We make sure we're all ready when it goes down and keep her away from Penny by running interference for her." The others could see the cogs turn in Rob's mind as he spoke.

"I think Frances needs to know about it." Alex frowned.

"We can do it without her knowing Alex, no need to spoil her big day."

"No, Bernie, you don't understand; Frances needs to know because she'd give her eye teeth to see Laura get what's coming to her."

"Okay we tell Frances, then what do we do?" Ash queried.

"I guess I'll go and look for Penny and bring her here. She wants to see me, so I'll oblige her. Rob, you go talk to Frances and bring her here in, say, fifteen minutes. Bernie, you do the same to Millie. I'll make sure Laura sees Penny and I leave the dining room and follows us out. When I'm done with Penny in here, I'll leave the way clear for Laura. That's when we move in and sort this out for good." The others nodded as Alex gave them their marching orders.

Penny had returned to her table and was busy wiping Rose's hands with a face wipe when Alex went ahead of Bernie and leaned over to whisper in her ear. A second later she stood up and followed him out of the room. Laura watched them and when they'd disappeared through the door she got to her feet and followed them.

Inside the room Penny was standing quietly as Alex settled a hip against the edge of a table. She wanted to talk to him but now they were alone she didn't know how to start.

"How have you both been?" Alex asked as his eyes settled on Rose, but Rose wouldn't look at him and it was slightly upsetting him.

"Fine." Penny sighed.

"I was told you wanted to talk so..."

"Yes." She cleared her throat, then winced when she adjusted Rose in her arms.

"You hurt?" Alex reached out for Penny's hand but she kept it away from him.

"It's nothing..." Penny's eyes closed briefly as she puffed out another sigh.

"I have three things I want to say. One. Here's your ring, I know it's very special to you, so I want you to have it back."

She was holding the band out to him and dropped it into his palm when he raised his hand.

"Two. Rose missed you. She still does, I think. If you want to continue seeing her you can, but don't hurt her, be constant not indifferent."

"Penny."

"We can work things out later, when you're sure about what you want." Penny continued.

"Penny? Are you okay?"

"I'm talking to you about our daughter while a lunatic is

somewhere close by just waiting for a chance to hurt her and me, or just me. So, no I'm not alright."

"We won't let her hurt you anymore Penny."

Penny sighed as she set Rose on the floor.

"She's like a damn ninja, one minute you're enjoying life and the next she creeps out from the shadows and gives you a reality check."

"Did she hurt Rose?"

"Doused her in pink wine and made her have a wash, which she hates, but nothing else."

"Good. What's the third thing you want to tell me."

(Oh Lord. Number three!)

"Number three. I have to tell you something important. Something I think you deserve to know; you don't have to feel like you owe me anything or need to be there or anything like that. I just think you should know that's all."

(She had another man. She wanted the divorce he once demanded! She...)

"I'm pregnant again. I can't believe it, but I can."

Penny shook her head to try to clear it.

"I'm not after anything, not your money or your time or you I just want you to know that's it."

He didn't say anything, so she picked up her daughter, settled her on her hip and started for the door.

"Penny?"

She ignored him.

"Penny, wait."

She stopped walking but didn't turn to face him.

"I have three things I want to say to you.

(Okay. Only fair.)

Penny turned round.

"One. This ring is yours; I want you to wear it, all the time. I have one of my own and I promise to honour you by wearing it for the rest of my life."

Alex slipped the ring back onto her finger and then held her hand in his.

"Two. Rose is my daughter; I want her in my life always because I love her as much as I love her mother.

Three. I'm not about to let you leave me without a fight; I want to be there for our baby and Rose, I want to see them every day, I want to make love to you every night. I'm excited. Really excited, because I have a beautiful daughter and an unborn child who I want to see growing inside you. I want to be there when it's born and look after it forever. And finally, I want to kiss you, because I just want to."

He paused.

"That's it, that's all I have to say, what do you think?"

"I think I want to kiss you too. I think Rose will love having her dad around and I think the new baby will love it too."

He kissed her. Then kissed her again and then he took Rose from her and told her what was going to happen next.

Five minutes later Alex manufactured a frown then walked out of the room and left the door open behind him. Laura was watching through a crack in the opposite doorway and saw him leave; she was smiling as she pulled the door open and began to walk across the corridor, towards Penny and her little monster.

"Alone again Jane." Laura crooned as she entered then moved quickly into the room and closed the door.

"Tsk, tsk, not very good at the bodyguard stuff, are they?"

Penny didn't respond, she fastened Rose onto her hip and just watched and moved, keeping a good amount of space between her and her tormentor

"So, who's the daddy of your little bastard?"

Laura was frowning as her eyes flicked around the room.

(Probably hoping a window was open.)

"I know it isn't Alex. He can't stand you. I loved it when you blamed him for knocking you off that stool."

"I already apologised to him for that." Penny lied.

"Really? So, you knew it was me?"

"When I took the time to think about it, yes. Just like it was you who put the suitcase behind me at the airport."

"So, who is the daddy of your little leech?"

Laura had caught up to her and tried to catch Rose by the chin. Penny shifted her quickly then winced as her wrist screamed against the movement.

"Oh, is it sore? Let me make it worse for you!"

"Penny? You, okay?" Frances walked into the room, followed closely by Alex and Rob, Georgia and Millie and Bernie and Ashley.

"We're just having a little chat." Laura told them as her eyes landed on Ashley and her mouth gave him a blatantly flirty smile.

"Hello Ashley darling" she crooned at him "I've missed you in my bed."

Ashley didn't reply. He was only there to give Frances his undying love and support.

Frances, however, had things to say that had been kept inside for too long.

"Laura Taylor, how on earth did you get into my wedding reception?" Frances asked as she glared at the female.

Georgia and Millie knew but said nothing.

"And why have you come?" she continued.

"I'm with Orson Black."

"WHO?" Frances and Ashley looked at each other.

"The director Orson Black. He's going to be big on Broadway soon." Laura boasted.

"Never heard of him." chorused the friends.

"It doesn't matter, what does matter is who is the daddy of Penny's little bastard. Don't you all just want to know? I know I do."

(They did actually but it wasn't keeping them awake at night.)

"Why are you so interested?"

Frances was beginning to think that Laura was not dealing from a full deck.

"Because I probably had him in my bed first, like I nearly had you Alex, I just want to know who it is that brought the prim and proper Penelope Craig down to the level of a whore."

"That's it I'm going to deck her!" Millie tried to get past her husband, but he was holding onto her fast and steady.

"I'm not a whore Laura."

"Looks like you are."

"And Rose isn't a child born out of wedlock." Alex admitted.

All eyes moved onto him, but Alex was unfazed.

"Oh, dear you've all bought into the idea that Penny is all white and virginal." Laura hissed.

"She's a bit of a tree hugger." Bertie mused.

"And not at all a clothes horse." Ashley added.

"And a great mum and sister." Rob smiled.

"And a sexy wife." Alex smiled at Penny and her heartbeat increased. Everyone else went quiet as the conversation changed, became one between Alex and Laura, and a short one at that.

"You're a stupid man Alex Sterling. Jane is no more married than I am the queen."

"Laura."

Alex walked past her and caught Penny by the waist then slipped his hand over her stomach.

"I may look stupid, but I know this. If you ever touch my wife and kids again, I'll have you arrested for GBH."

"Hallelujah." Frances shouted as she grinned at her brother. Then she remembered Laura and turned her attention onto her.

"You need to take your budding director and leave before I

have you thrown out..." Frances paused then growled... "You have five minutes."

Laura left.

Frances hugged her brother and everyone else laughed as the tension slipped out of the door after Laura.

"You're married." Georgia was grinning. "When did that happen?"

"The first night in Vegas." Alex and Penny said almost in unison.

"Really? That long ago?" Rob's eyebrows went into his hairline.

"Yeah."

"You did it in a wedding chapel?" Bernie grinned.

Penny nodded.

"Which one?" Georgia gushed.

Rob didn't look pleased.

"Not the one down the road from the hotel." He asked hoping that it wasn't.

"The one with the old guy who looked like a vampire?" Bertie asked looking perplexed

"More likely the one with the man with the great hair and glitter suit." Offered Millie. "You know how mad Penny is about him, so it has to be him... right?"

"No, not him..." Penny tipped her head and frowned. "I'm not sure how we ended up there, I just kind of followed Alex really, who kind of followed someone else... anyway" Penny was flapping her hands.

"We ended up in this really lovely place... and Dusti was soo sweet... she let me see her tiara and told me about her grand-mother and she asked me if I liked Alex and of course I said I Do."

"And then she asked me if I wanted Penny and of course I said I Do too." Added Alex quickly.

"And then we signed the paper and that was how it happened." Offered Penny as she gazed at Alex.

"Yeah…" Alex gave Penny a soft, sexy smile that melted her heart.

"And now there will be four of us." Whispered Penny as she pressed her lips to Alex's.

"Really?"

Millie kissed Bernie on the mouth and her daughter on top of her head.

"Us too!"

"Ditto." Georgia grinned as she caught hold of Rob's arm.

"Isn't this great? All of the maids and groomsmen got married to each other and now they're going to be mums and dads again. Roll on next year."

"Um."

Frances smiled as they all looked in her direction.

"I'd just like to add that some of us are going to be parents for the first time and will need lots of advice and help getting used to it."

The women squealed, then ended up in a bouncing huddle as they congratulated Frances and each other for their good news.

The men simply shook each other's hand as everyone silently agreed that it would take a long time to come to terms with the fact that Penny and Alex had been married the longest and even longer to learn the true circumstances of their first year as man and wife.

20

THE END... OR IS IT THE BEGINNING?

Rose was sitting on the floor surrounded by packages covered in brightly coloured paper. It was her second Christmas, and she was a little less confused by it than she had been by the first. The best part of it was that that man Alex had stayed over and was in her mummy's bed. She liked him; he made her feel safe when he held her, just like mummy did.

Maybe she'd call him da. It would be a nice name for him.

Elena was in her element. Both the eldest grandchildren were sitting on the floor looking a little overawed by the packages and ribbons.

The Turkey had been in the oven for the past two hours, cooking slowly surrounded by onions and covered by a large piece of cooking foil.

Henry was making her a cup of tea and upstairs; Rob and Georgia were still in bed enjoying their second Christmas together.

And then there was also Penny, and Alex.

They'd finally admitted that they loved each other and were making the most of their first night and morning as man and wife (proper.)

The day was going to be perfect.

The coming year was going to be great.

Yes, things were going to change but when the rearrangements and buildings were completed, they were going to go from strength to strength, because their family was growing and so was the love they had for each other.

Roll on the New Year.

Elena couldn't wait.

Penny had woken up naked again. Her head was functioning normally, no headache. Her stomach was as it had been the last time, she was three months pregnant, and her feminine bits were just orgasmic.

Someone was kissing her, along the silver scar on her side and then across her belly.

(The moist feel of a tongue could do soo many things to a female libido, and it was.)

The hand that touched her breast was firm and insistent, so was the tongue that laved her nipple and sucked it firm.

She was sinking into the quicksand of lust and desire and wished that Alex would move his mouth onto hers.

He didn't, he brought his leg up instead, and eased it between her thighs making her move them to make space for him. He was above her now, his lovely face inches from hers, his hands either side of her face. She felt his foot touch hers and she caught it between her own.

It wasn't such a bad foot, she thought as her toes ran across the top of it, feeling the coarse hair that lay on its surface.

Not so bad at all.

Penny kissed him quickly then put a finger on his lips to stop him when he moved to follow up on it.

"I love you, big foot with the pointy elbows." She whispered.

"I love you too tree hugger." He whispered back.

"Are you ready?" she smiled.

"Yes."

He kissed her gently on the mouth.

"Then lets... hmmm."

He entered her body as he kissed her again and they were soon lost in each other as they moved together.

Meanwhile downstairs Elena had put on her Christmas playlist, and was singing along with 80's pop music as she danced around the sitting room holding Rose.

And then they were both laughing because that's what Christmas was about.

Family and love and laughter.

And today the house would be full to the brim with it all.

The End.

(Or is it?)

BUT WHAT HAPPENS NEXT?

Subscribe to my Newsletter and receive a free download of
The Wedding Party Epilogue:

**Find Out What Happened in Vegas
10 Months Later!**

Scan the QR code with your phone camera to be taken to the
sign up!
www.jeanmartin.co.uk/free-extra-wp

Subscribe to stay in the loop for more Photography, Writing
and Creative releases!

Excerpt of Ginny Martin - A Love Through Time

1716 THE LOVERS CURSED

May 25th, 1716

He was tall and well built. His hair was black as black, and his chest was broad enough for her head to rest upon as her hands touched and caressed it.

He was her idea of a man, all muscle and dark good looks.

Strong hands and arms and soft kissable lips.

She was smitten when she saw him approach her father who was labouring in a new pasture he had just acquired, marking out the ground for the dimensions of a cottage.

Ginny did not know what a cottage looked like for all the homes about them were round structures with thatched rooves; this 'cottage' must be something different. Just like this man was different to those other men who were born in the country.

Anyway. He walked up to her father, bold as brass, and asked for work. Now, she knew her father never employed anyone to help with the building of anything.

Not a wall.

Not a chimney.

And certainly not a new-fangled 'cottage' that, he declared nightly, was going to be the new home for country folk; with its long walls and corners and small windows and pointed thatched roof.

No, he never employed anyone for he had two strapping sons who could do the work with him and for him so this 'Goliath of a beautiful man' would not be successful here today or on any other day.

Well now.

Ginny had watched as the young man asked for work and was more than a little surprised when a smile broke out on his face when her father shook his hand and bade him to be there to start work the next morning.

No one was more surprised than Ginny that this 'Happening' had happened.

No one was more pleased than Ginny that it had, for she was already smitten, and she could not have lived as before if he had been sent on his way.

Yes. Her father had taken him on to work and work he would and that meant that Ginny would not be absent from the field anymore. For she would not be, not when there was this man to feast her eyes upon.

And feast she did, as she smiled shyly at him when he looked at her more often with each passing day.

And that was how it began.

With his working for her da and her infatuation with him.

With his loving her...and leaving her.

Then the farce of a wedding and the words uttered in anger and frustration.

The start was quick and sure but the ending was somewhat different for she did not know now that the whole damn mess of it would follow her far into the future...

The Story Continues...
2023

Ginny Martin - A Love Through Time

Please Visit **www.jeanmartin.co.uk** for more information on her books and upcoming releases...
OR
Sign up to her Reader Group & Newsletter at:
www.jeanmartin.co.uk/weddingparty
To be kept in the loop with updates direct from her writer's desk...

ACKNOWLEDGMENTS

I'd like to thank my daughters Elizabeth and Victoria for their constant love and support in my creative endeavours and in life. This first step into writing would not exist without the two of you thank you for helping me achieve my dream.

I'd also like to thank Laura Wilkinson for her encouragement and her ability to make me believe in my talents and in myself. I would not have had the confidence to take this step without her help.

And to my Aggie for being a fluffy ball of carnage and love.

FOLLOW ME

Follow Jean Martin to stay in the loop for more Photography, Writing and Creative releases!

Subscribe to her News Letter
www.jeanmartin.co.uk/weddingparty

Website
www.jeanmartin.co.uk

Blog
www.jeanmartin.co.uk/blog

Facebook
www.facebook.com/Jeanmartinauthor

Instagram
www.instagram.com/Jeanmartinauthor

ABOUT THE AUTHOR

Jean Martin has loved writing and books for as long as she can remember.

She has written poetry, historical and modern romance as a hobby alongside her retail work and amateur photography.

As a child she travelled with her parents and was born in Singapore due to her father being in the army before they settled in a coastal Kentish town.

It is here that she still resides today walking, writing, working and capturing nature with her camera.

Follow My Daughters

They helped create this book

ELIZABETH CLARK

INSPIRATIONAL ARTISTRY

FINE ARTIST

WWW.ELIZABETHMJCLARK.COM

Victoria Clark

ARTISAN YARN

 @Fox_trot_yarns

CPSIA information can be obtained
at www.ICGtesting.com
Printed in the USA
BVHW051240271122
652780BV00012BA/1026